Sylvie turned to find her way blocked by six and a half feet of broad-shouldered male, and experienced a bewildering sense of déjà vu.

A definite feeling that this had happened before.

And then she looked up and realized it was not an illusion. This *had* happened before—except on that occasion the male concerned had been wearing navy pinstripe instead of gray cashmere.

"Some billionaire…" her friend had said, but hadn't mentioned a name. And Sylvie hadn't bothered to ask, pretending she didn't care.

She cared now, because it wasn't just "some" billionaire who'd bought her family home and was planning to turn it into a conference center.

It was Tom McFarlane, the man with whom—just for a few moments—she'd totally lost it. The man whose baby she was carrying.

A *Bride* FOR ALL *Seasons*

Would your perfect wedding be in the **spring,**
when flowers are starting to blossom and
it's the perfect season for new beginnings?

Or perhaps a balmy garden wedding,
set off by a riot of color that makes the
summer bride glow with the joys of a happy future?

Do you dream of being a **fall** bride,
who walks down the aisle amid the dazzling reds
and burnished golds of falling leaves?

Or of a **winter** wedding dusted with glistening white
snowflakes, celebrated by the ringing of
frosty church bells?

With Harlequin Romance® you can have them all!
And, best of all, you can experience the
rush of falling in love with a gorgeous groom....

This month:
The Bride's Baby by Liz Fielding

Look out for:
Saying Yes to the Millionaire by Fiona Harper in June!
The Millionaire's Proposal by Trish Wylie in September
Marry-Me Christmas by Shirley Jump in December

LIZ FIELDING

The Bride's Baby

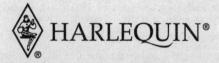

TORONTO • NEW YORK • LONDON
AMSTERDAM • PARIS • SYDNEY • HAMBURG
STOCKHOLM • ATHENS • TOKYO • MILAN • MADRID
PRAGUE • WARSAW • BUDAPEST • AUCKLAND

ISBN-13: 978-0-373-17506-2
ISBN-10:   0-373-17506-X

THE BRIDE'S BABY

First North American Publication 2008.

Copyright © 2008 by Liz Fielding.

www.eHarlequin.com

Printed in U.S.A.

Liz Fielding was born with itchy feet. She made it to Zambia before her twenty-first birthday and, gathering her own special hero and a couple of children on the way, lived in Botswana, Kenya and Bahrain—with pauses for sightseeing pretty much everywhere in between. She finally came to a full stop in a tiny Welsh village cradled by misty hills, and these days mostly leaves her pen to do the traveling. When she's not sorting out the lives and loves of her characters, she potters in the garden, reads her favorite authors and spends a lot of time wondering "What if…?" For news of upcoming books—and to sign up for her occasional newsletter—visit Liz's Web site at www.lizfielding.com.

"Liz Fielding's *The Sheikh's Unsuitable Bride* has it all— irresistible characters…along with oodles of sizzle and witty banter. Pure magic from the beginning to end."
—*Romantic Times BOOKreviews*

CHAPTER ONE

SYLVIE SMITH checked the time. Her appointment had been for
two o'clock. The time on her laptop now read two forty-five—
because she hadn't just sat there in the luxurious reception of
Tom McFarlane's penthouse office suite twiddling her thumbs
and drinking coffee.

Chance would have been a fine thing.

The message couldn't have been plainer.

She was the enemy and so she'd been left to twiddle her thumbs
without the courtesy of a cup of coffee to help fill the time.

Not a problem. Her nerves were already in shreds without
adding a surfeit of caffeine to the mix. And she hadn't twiddled
her thumbs either. She didn't have time to waste thumb-twid-
dling. Didn't have time to waste, full stop.

Instead she'd occupied herself finalising the details of an
Indian-style wedding she was coordinating for a supermodel.
She'd even managed to track down an elephant that was for hire
by the day.

She'd also soothed the nerves of a fading pop diva who was
hoping to revive her career with a spectacular launch party for
her new album.

All of which had helped to keep her from dwelling upon the
approaching meeting. When—if—it ever happened.

She knew she was the last person in the world Tom McFarlane wanted to see. Understood why he'd want to put off the moment for as long as was humanly possible. The feeling was mutual.

The only thing she didn't understand was why, when he'd been so obviously avoiding her for the last six months, he was putting them both through this now.

She checked the time again. Ten to three. Enough was enough. Her patience might be limitless—it was that, and her attention to detail, that made her one of the most sought-after event planners in London—but her time was not.

This meeting had been Tom McFarlane's idea. The very last thing she'd wanted was a meeting with a man she hadn't been able to get out of her mind since she'd first set eyes on him. A man who had been about to marry her old school friend, and darling of the gossip mags, Candida Harcourt.

All she wanted was his cheque so that she could settle outstanding bills and put the whole sorry nightmare behind her.

She closed down her laptop, packed it away, then crossed to the desk and the receptionist who had been studiously ignoring her ever since she'd arrived.

'I can't wait any longer,' she said. 'Please tell Mr McFarlane that I'll be in my office after ten o'clock tomorrow if he has any queries on the account.'

'Oh, but—'

'I should already be somewhere else,' she said, cutting short the woman's protest. Not strictly true—her staff were more than capable of dealing with any crisis involving the album launch party, but sometimes you had to make the point that your time— if not quite as valuable as that of a billionaire—was still a limited commodity. And maybe, on reflection, he'd be as glad as she was to avoid this confrontation and just put a cheque in the post. 'If I don't leave now—'

The receptionist didn't answer but a prickle of awareness as the woman's gaze shifted to somewhere over her right shoulder warned her that they were no longer alone.

Turning, she found her view blocked by a broad chest, wide shoulders encased in a white linen shirt. It was open at the neck and the sleeves had been rolled back to the elbow to reveal brawny forearms, strong wrists.

A silk tie had been pulled loose as if its owner had been wrestling with some intractable problem. She didn't doubt that, whatever it was, he'd won.

Despite the fact that she'd spent the last six months planning Tom McFarlane's wedding, this was only the second time she'd actually seen him face to face.

Make that forehead to chin, she thought, forced, despite her highest heels, to look up. She'd known this was going to be a difficult afternoon and had felt the need to armour herself with serious clothes.

The chin was deeply cleft.

She already knew that. She'd seen photographs long before she'd met the man. Tom McFarlane wasn't much of a socialite, but no billionaire bachelor could entirely escape the attention of the gossip magazines, especially once his marriage to the daughter of a minor aristocrat—one who'd made a career out of appearing in the glossies—had been announced.

The cleft did nothing to undermine its force; on the contrary, it emphasised it and, for the second time, her only thought was, What on earth was Candy *thinking*?

Stupid question.

From the moment she'd bounced into her office demanding that SDS Events organise her wedding to billionaire businessman Tom McFarlane, Sylvie had known *exactly* what Candy had been thinking.

This was the fulfilment of her 'life plan'. The one with which, years ago, she'd enlivened a school careers seminar by announcing that her 'career plan' was to marry a millionaire. One with a house in Belgravia, a country estate and a title. The title was negotiable; one should apparently be *flexible*—the size of the bank account was not.

Why waste her time sweating over exams when she had no intention of going to university? Students saddled with overdrafts and loans held no interest for her. All her effort was going to be put into perfecting her natural assets—at which point she'd performed a pouty, cheesecake pose—and making the perfect marriage.

Everyone had laughed—that was the thing about Candy, she always made you laugh—but no one had actually doubted that she meant it, or that she was capable of achieving her goal.

She'd already looked like coming close a couple of times. Maybe, rising thirty, she'd realised that time was running out and she'd jettisoned everything but the core plan although, inflation being what it was, she'd upgraded her ambition to billionaire.

A better question might have been, What on earth had Tom McFarlane been thinking?

An even dumber question.

It was a truth universally acknowledged that a smile from Candy Harcourt's sexy mouth was enough to short-circuit the brain of any man who could muster more than one red blood cell. She might have bypassed her exams but she hadn't stinted on the midnight oil when it came to enhancing her career assets which were, it had to be admitted, considerable.

Gorgeous, funny—who could possibly resist her? Why would any man try?

And while Tom McFarlane might give the impression that he'd been rough-hewn from rock—and eyes that were, at that moment, glittering like granite certainly added to the impression of unyielding force—she had absolutely no doubt that he was a male with red blood cells to spare.

Something her own red blood cells had instantly responded to with the shocking eagerness of a puppy offered something unspeakable to roll in.

As their eyes had met over Candy's artfully tumbled blonde curls, the connection had short-circuited all those troublesome hormones which had been in cold storage for a decade and they'd instantly defrosted.

She was not a puppy, however, but a successful businesswoman and she'd made a determined effort to ignore the internal heatwave and stick to the matter in hand. Fortunately, the minute he'd signed her contract, Tom McFarlane—who obviously had much more important things to do—had made his excuses and left.

Just thinking about those ten long minutes left the silk of the camisole she was wearing beneath her linen jacket sticking to her skin. But she'd got through it then and she could do it again.

It was part of the job. As an event planner she was used to handling awkward situations—and this certainly came under the heading of 'awkward'. She just needed to concentrate on business, even if, feeling a little like the space between the rock and the hard place, it took all her composure to stiffen her knees, stand her ground, keep the expression neutral.

'If you don't leave now?' he prompted.

'I'll be in trouble…' Wrong. She was already in trouble, but with the hardwood reception desk at her back and the rock blocking her exit she was stuck with it. Reminding herself that drooling was a very bad look, she summoned up a professional smile and extended a hand. 'Good afternoon, Mr McFarlane. I was just explaining to your receptionist—'

'I heard.' He ignored the hand. 'Call whoever's expecting you and tell him he'll have to wait. You're mine until I say otherwise.'

What? That was outrageous but the glitter in those eyes warned her that provocation had been his intent. That he was waiting for the explosion. That he would welcome it.

Not in this life, she thought, managing a fairly creditable, 'She. Delores Castello,' she added, naming the pop diva. 'So you'll see why your request is quite impossible.' She wanted this over and done with, not dragged out, but when a man started tossing orders around as if he owned the world, it was a woman's duty to stand her ground and prove to him that he did not.

Even if the knees had other ideas.

'I do have a window in my diary,' she began, flipping open the side pocket of her bag.

If she'd hoped to impress him with her client list the strategy signally failed. Before she could locate her diary he said, 'What's impossible, Miss Smith, is the chance of you getting another chance to talk me into settling your outrageous account.'

Sylvie grabbed her bottom lip with her teeth before she said something she'd regret.

The man was angry. She understood that. But her account was not outrageous. On the contrary, she'd worked really hard to negotiate the best possible cancellation deals, pushing people to the limit. She hadn't had to do that but she had felt just the smallest bit *responsible* for what had happened.

She would have told him so if her lip hadn't been clamped between her teeth.

'Your call, Miss Smith,' he prompted, apparently convinced that he'd proved his point. 'But if you walk away now I promise you you're going to have to sue me all the way to the House of Lords to get your money.'

He had to be kidding.

Or, then again, maybe not.

Glacial, his voice went with the raw cheekbones, jutting nose, a mouth compressed into a straight line. It did nothing to cool her. Like a snow-capped volcano she knew that, deep beneath the surface, molten lava bubbled dangerously. That if she wasn't careful the heat would be terminal.

Tom McFarlane was made from the same stuff that centuries ago had driven men across uncharted oceans in search of glory and fortune. He was their modern equivalent—a twenty-first-century legend who'd worked in the markets as a boy, had been trading wholesale by the time he'd been in his teens, making six-figure deals by the time he'd left school. His first million by the time he'd been twenty. The expression 'self-made man' could have been invented just for him.

He was the genuine article, no doubt, but, much as she admired that kind of drive and tenacity, his humble beginnings had made him a very odd choice of mate for Candy.

He might be a billionaire but he had none of the trappings of old money. None of the grace. He wasn't a man to sit back and idle his time away playing the squire.

There was no country estate or smart London town house. Just a vast loft apartment which, according to an exasperated Candy, was on the wrong side of the river.

Apparently, when she'd pointed that out to him, he'd laughed, ridiculing those who paid a fortune for a classy address to look across the river at him.

She'd been forced to hide a smile herself when Candy had told her that. Had thought, privately, that there had to be billionaires out there who would be less abrasive, easier to handle.

But maybe not quite so much of a challenge.

The chase might have been chillingly calculated but Sylvie was pretty sure that when the quarry had been run to earth and the prize claimed, the result would have been hot as Hades.

Maybe Candy was, when it came right down to it, as human as the next woman and had fallen not for the money, but for the testosterone.

The fact that Tom McFarlane had exactly the same effect on her, Sylvie thought as, not waiting for her answer, he turned and walked across reception to the wide-open doors of his office—leaving her to follow or not, as she chose—did not make her feel one whit better.

On the contrary.

But if Candy had thought she'd got him where she wanted him, she'd been fooling herself.

She might have momentarily brought him to heel with her silicone-enhanced assets but he wasn't the man to dance on her lead for long.

Unlike his bride, however, Sylvie wasn't in any position to cut and run when the going got tough. This wasn't 'her' money. Her account was mostly made up of invoices from dozens of small companies—single traders who'd done their job. People who were relying on her. And, sending a stern message to her brain to stay on message, she went through the motions of calling her very confused assistant and explaining that she would be late.

The call took no more than thirty seconds but, by the time she'd caught up with him, Tom McFarlane was already seated at his desk, a lick of thick, dark brown hair sliding over the lean, work-tempered fingers on which he'd propped his forehead as he concentrated on the folder in front of him.

An exact copy of the one that must have arrived in the same post as his bride's Dear John letter. The one he'd returned with the suggestion that she forward it to the new man in his ex-bride-to-be's life.

Except he hadn't been that polite.

She'd understood his reaction. Felt a certain amount of sympathy for the man.

She might honestly believe that he'd had a lucky escape, but obviously he didn't feel that way and he had every right to be hurt and angry. Being dumped just days before your wedding was humiliating, no matter who you were. Something she knew from first-hand experience.

She and Tom McFarlane had that in common, if nothing else, which was why she understood—no one better—that an expression of sympathy, an 'I know what you're going through' response, would not be welcome.

If she knew anything, it was that no one could have the slightest idea what he was feeling.

Instead, she'd tucked the account and the thick wad of copy invoices into a new folder—one of the SDS Events folders rather than another of the silver, wedding-bells adorned kind she used for weddings—and had returned it with a polite note reminding him that it was his signature on the contract and that the terms were payment within twenty-eight days.

She hadn't bothered to remind him that five of those days had already elapsed, or add, After which time I'll place the account in the hands of my solicitor…

She'd been confident that he'd get the subtext. Just as she'd been sure that he would understand, on reflection, that coordinating a wedding—even when you were doing it for an old school friend—was, like any other commercial enterprise, just business.

She'd hoped for a cheque by return. What she'd got was a call from the man himself, demanding she present herself at his office at two o'clock the next day.

She hadn't had a chance to tell him that her afternoon was already spoken for since, having issued his command, he'd hung up. Instead, she'd taken a deep breath and rescheduled her appointments. And been kept waiting the best part of an hour for her pains.

When she didn't immediately sit down, Tom McFarlane

glanced up and she felt a jolt—like the fizz of electricity from a faulty switch—as something dangerous sparked the silver specks buried in the granite-grey of his eyes. The same jolt that had passed between them on their first meeting. Hot slivers of lightning that heated her to the bone, bringing a flush to her cheeks, a tingle to parts of her anatomy that no other glance had reached since…no, forget since. She'd never felt that kind of response to any man. Not even Jeremy.

What on earth was the matter with her?

She'd never done anything at first sight. Certainly not love. She'd known Jeremy from her cradle. Actually, that might not have been the best example…

Whatever.

She certainly didn't intend to change the habits of a lifetime with *lust*. Mixing business with pleasure was always a mistake.

But it meant that she understand *exactly* what Candida had been thinking. Why she hadn't settled for some softer billionaire. Some malleable sugar daddy who would buy her the country estate and anything else she wanted…

'I'd advise you to sit down, Miss Smith,' he said. 'This is going to take some time.'

Usually, she and her clients were on first name terms from the word go but they had both clung firmly to formality at that first meeting and she didn't think this was the moment to respond with, *Sylvie, please…*

And since her knees, in their weakened state, had buckled in instant obedience to his command, she was too busy making sure her backside connected securely with the chair to cope with something as complicated as speech at the same time.

He watched as she wriggled to locate the safety of the centre of the chair. Continued to watch her for what seemed like endless moments.

The heat intensified and, without thinking, she slipped the buttons on her jacket.

Only when she was completely still and he was certain that he had her attention—although why it had taken him so long to realise *that* she couldn't possibly imagine; he'd had her absolute attention from the moment she'd set eyes on him— did he speak.

'Have you sacked him?' he demanded. 'The Honourable Quentin Turner Lyall.'

She swallowed. Truth, dare… She stopped right there and went for the truth.

'As I'm sure you're aware,' she said, 'falling in love is not grounds for dismissal. I have no doubt that the Employment Tribunal would take me to the cleaners if I tried.'

'Love?' he repeated, as if it were a dirty word.

'What else?' she asked. What else would have made Candy run for the hills when she had the prize within days of her grasp?

She had Tom McFarlane, so presumably she had the lust thing covered…

But, having dismissed her question with an impatient gesture, he said, 'What about duty of care to your client, Miss Smith? In your letter you did make the point that I am your client.' He regarded her stonily. 'And I imagine Mr Lyall did go absent without leave?'

Oh, Lord! 'Actually, he… No. He asked me for some time off…'

He sat back, apparently speechless.

'Are you telling me you actually gave him leave to elope with a woman whose wedding you were arranging?' he said, after what felt like the longest pause in history.

This was probably not a good time to give him the 'dying grandmother' excuse that she'd fallen for.

When Candy had borrowed Quentin for bag-carrying duties on one of her many shopping expeditions it had never crossed Sylvie's mind that she'd risk her big day with the billionaire for a fling with a twenty-five-year-old events assistant. Even one who'd eventually make her a countess. He came from a long-lived family and the chances of him succeeding to his grandfather's earldom before he was fifty—more likely sixty—were remote.

And, while she'd been absolutely furious with both of them, she did have a certain sympathy for Quentin; if a man like Tom McFarlane had succumbed to Candy's 'assets', what hope was there for an innocent like him?

But, despite what she'd told Tom McFarlane, when Candy had finished with Quentin and he did eventually return, she was going to have explain that, under the circumstances, he couldn't possibly continue working for her. Bad enough that it would feel like kicking a puppy, but Quentin was a real asset and losing him was going to hurt. He had a real gift for calming neurotic women. He was also thoroughly decent. It would never occur to him to go to a tribunal for unfair dismissal.

Maybe it was calming Candy's pre-wedding nerves—she had gone into shopping overdrive in those last few weeks—that broad sympathetic shoulder of his, that had got him into so much trouble in the first place.

Tom McFarlane, however, having fired off this last salvo, had returned to the folder in front of him and was flicking through the invoices, stopping to glance at one occasionally, his face utterly devoid of expression.

Sylvie didn't say a word. She just waited, holding her breath. Watching his long fingers as they turned the pages. She could no longer see his eyes. Just the edge of his jaw. The shadowy cleft of his chin. A corner of that hard mouth…

The only sound in the office was the slow turning of paper

as Tom McFarlane confronted the ruin of his plans—marriage to a woman whose family tree could be traced back to William the Conqueror.

That, and the ragged breathing of the woman opposite him.

She was nervous. And so she should be.

He had never been so angry.

His marriage to the aristocratic Candida Harcourt would have been the culmination of all his ambitions. With her as his wife, he would have finally shaken off the last remnants of the world from which he'd dragged himself.

Would have attained everything that the angry youth he'd once been had sworn would one day be his.

The good clothes, expensive cars, beautiful women had come swiftly, but this had been something else.

He hadn't been foolish enough to believe that Candy had fallen in love with him—love caused nothing but heartache and pain, as he knew to his cost—but it had seemed like the perfect match. She'd had everything except money; he had more than enough of that to indulge her wildest dreams.

It had been while he was away securing the biggest of those—guilt, perhaps for the fact that he'd been unable to get her wedding planner out of his head—that she'd taken to her heels with the chinless wonder who was reduced to working as an events assistant to keep a roof over his head. How ironic was that?

But then he was an *aristocratic* chinless wonder.

The coronet always cancelled out the billions.

When it came down to it, class won. Sylvie Smith had, after all, been chosen to coordinate the wedding for no better reason than that she'd been to school with Candy.

That exclusive old boy network worked just as well for women, it seemed.

Sylvie Smith. He'd spent six months trying not to think

about her. An hour trying to make himself send her away without seeing her.

As he appeared to concentrate on the papers in front of him, she slipped the buttons on her jacket to reveal something skimpy in dark brown silk barely skimming breasts that needed no silicone to enhance them, nervously pushed back a loose strand of dark blonde hair that was, he had no doubt, the colour she'd been born with.

She crossed her legs in order to prop up the folder she had on her knee and for a moment he found himself distracted by a classy ankle, a long slender foot encased in a dark brown suede peep-toe shoe that was decorated with a saucy bow.

And, without warning, she wasn't the only one feeling the heat.

He should write a cheque now. Get her out of his office. Instead, he dropped his eyes to the invoice in front of him and snapped, 'What in the name of blazes is a confetti cannon?'

'A c-confetti c-cannon?'

Sylvie's mind spun like a disengaged gear. Going nowhere. She'd thought this afternoon couldn't get any worse; she'd been wrong. Time to get a grip, she warned herself. Take it one thing at a time. And remember to breathe.

Maybe lighten things up a little. 'Actually, it does what it says on the tin,' she said.

His eyebrows rose the merest fraction. 'Which is?'

Or maybe not.

'It fires a cannonade of c-confetti,' she stuttered. Dammit, she hadn't stuttered in years and she wasn't about to start again now just because Tom McFarlane was having a bad day. Slow, slow…'In all shapes and sizes,' she finished carefully.

He said nothing.

'With a c-coloured flame projector,' she added, unnerved by the silence. 'It's really quite…' she faltered '…spectacular.'

He was regarding her as if she were mad. Actually, she thought with a tiny shiver, he might just be right. What sane person spent her time scouring the Internet looking for an elephant to hire by the day?

Whose career highs involved delivering the perfect party for a pop star?

Easy. The kind of person who'd been doing it practically from her cradle. Whose mother had done it before her—although she'd done it out of love for family members or a sense of duty when it was for community events, rather than for money. The kind of person who, like Candy, hadn't planned for a day job but who'd fallen into it by chance and had been grateful to find something she could do without thinking, or the need for any specialist training.

'And a "field of light"?' he prompted, having apparently got the bit between his teeth.

'Thousands of strands of fibre optic lights that ripple in the breeze,' she answered, deciding this time to take the safe option and go for the straight answer. Then, since he seemed to require more, 'Changing colour as they move.'

She rippled her fingers to give him the effect.

He stared at them for a moment, then, snapping his gaze back to her face, said, 'What happens if there isn't a breeze?'

Did it matter? It wasn't going to happen...

Just answer the question, Sylvie, she told herself. 'The c-contractor uses fans.'

'You are joking.'

Describing the effect to someone who was anticipating a thrilling spectacle on her wedding day was a world away from explaining it to a man who thought the whole thing was some ghastly joke.

'Didn't you discuss any of this with Candy?' she asked.

His broad forehead creased in a frown. Another stupid question, obviously. You didn't become a billionaire by wasting time on trivialities like confetti cannons.

Tom McFarlane had signed the equivalent of a blank cheque and left his bride-to-be to organise the wedding of her dreams while he'd concentrated on making the money to pay for it.

No doubt, from Candy's point of view, it had been the perfect division of labour. She'd certainly thrown herself into her role with enthusiasm and there wasn't a single 'effect' that had gone unexplored. It was only the constraints of time and imagination—if she'd thought of an elephant, she'd have insisted on having one, insisted on having the whole damn circus—that had limited her self-indulgence. As it was, there had been more than enough to turn her dream into what was now proving to be Tom McFarlane's—and her—nightmare.

A six-figure nightmare, much of it provided by the small specialist companies Sylvie regularly did business with—people who trusted her to settle promptly. Which was why she was going to sit here until Tom McFarlane had worked through his anger and written her a cheque. Even if it took all night.

Having briefly recovered her equilibrium, she felt herself begin to heat up again, from the inside, as he continued to look at her and she began to think that, actually, all night wouldn't be a problem…

She ducked her head, as if to check the invoice, tucking a non-existent strand of hair behind her ear with a hand that was shaking slightly.

Tidying away what was a totally inappropriate thought.

Quentin wasn't the only one in danger of losing his head.

The office was oddly silent. His phone did not ring. No one put their head around the door with some query.

The only sound for what seemed like minutes—but was

probably only seconds—was the pounding beat of her pulse in her ears.

Then she heard the rustle of paper as Tom McFarlane returned to the stack of invoices in front of him and started going through them, one by one.

The choir.

'They didn't sing,' he objected. 'They didn't even have to turn up.'

'They're booked for months in advance,' she explained. 'I had to call in several favours to get them for Candy but the cancellation came too late to offload them to another booking...'

Her voice trailed off. He knew how it was, for heaven's sake; she shouldn't have to explain!

As if he could read her mind, he placed a tick against the list to approve payment without another word.

The bell-ringers.

For a moment she thought he was going to repeat his objection and held her breath. He glanced up, as if waiting for her to breathe out. Finally, when she was beginning to feel light-headed for lack of oxygen, he placed another tick.

As they moved steadily through the list, she began to relax. She hadn't doubted that he was going to settle; he wouldn't waste this amount of time unless he was going to pay.

The 1936 Rolls-Royce to carry Candy to the church. Tick.

It was just that he was angry and, since his runaway bride wasn't around to take the flak in person, she was being put through the wringer in her place.

If that was what it took, she thought, absent-mindedly fanning herself with one of her invoices, let him wring away. She could take it. Probably.

The carriage and pair to transport the newly-weds from the church to their reception. Tick.

The singing waiters...

Enough. Tom raked his fingers through his hair. He'd had enough. But, on the point of calling it quits, writing the cheque and drawing a line under the whole sorry experience, he looked up and was distracted by Sylvie Smith, her cheeks flushed a delicate pink, fanning herself with one of her outrageous invoices.

'Is it too warm in here for you, Miss Smith?' he enquired.

'No, I'm fine,' she said, quickly tucking the invoice away as she shifted the folder on her knees, tugging at her narrow skirt before re-crossing her long legs. Keeping her head down so that she wouldn't have to look at him. Waiting for him to get on with it so that she could escape.

Not yet, he thought, standing up, crossing to the water-cooler to fill a glass with iced water. Not yet...

Sylvie heard the creak of his leather chair as Tom McFarlane stood up. Then, moments later, the gurgle of water. Unable to help herself, she pushed her tongue between her dry lips, then looked up. For a moment he didn't move.

With the light behind him, she couldn't see his face, but his dark hair, perfectly groomed on that morning six months ago when he'd come to her office, never less than perfectly groomed in the photographs she'd seen of him before or since, looked as if he'd spent the last few days dragging his fingers through it.

Her fingers itched to smooth it back into place. To ease the tension from his wide shoulders and make the world right for him again. But the atmosphere in the silent office, cut off, high above London, was super-charged with suppressed emotion. Instead, she forced herself to look away, concentrate on the papers in front of her, well aware that all it would take would be a wrong word, move, look, to detonate an explosion.

'Here. Maybe this will help.'

She'd been working so hard at not looking at him that she

hadn't heard him cross the thick carpet. Now she looked up with a start to find him offering her a glass of water, presenting her with the added difficulty of taking it from his fingers without actually touching them.

A difficulty which something in his expression suggested he understood only too well. Maybe she should just ask him to do them both a favour and tip it over her…

'Thank you,' she said, reaching for it and to hell with the consequences. His were rock-steady—well, he was granite. Hers shook and she spilt a few drops on her skirt. She probably just imagined the steam as it soaked through the linen to her thighs as he folded himself down to her level and put his hand round hers to steady it.

Someone should warn him that it didn't actually help. But then she suspected he knew that too and right now she was having enough trouble simply breathing.

'I've got it,' she managed finally. He didn't appear to be convinced and she looked up, straight into his eyes, at which point the last thing she wanted was for him to let go. 'Really,' she assured him and instantly regretted it as he stood up and returned to his chair, lean and lithe as a panther.

And twice as dangerous, she thought as she gratefully took a sip of the water. Touched the glass to her heated forehead. Told herself to get a grip….

CHAPTER TWO

'SHALL we get on?' Tom McFarlane prompted as he returned to his desk.

Sylvie silently fumed.

Why on earth was he putting himself through this? Putting *her* through it?

It couldn't be about the money. The amount involved, though admittedly large, had to be peanuts to a man of his wealth.

It was almost, she thought, as if with each tick approving payment he was underlining the lesson he'd just been handed—the one about never trusting the word of someone just because they said they loved you. Presumably Candy *had* told him that she loved him. Or maybe, like Candy, he thought of marriage as a business deal, a mutually satisfying partnership arrangement. That love was just a lot of sentimental nonsense.

Maybe it wasn't his heart that was lying in shreds, but his pride. Or was it always pride that suffered most from this most public declaration that you weren't quite good enough?

'The singing waiters?' he repeated, making sure they were on the same page.

'I'm with you,' she said, putting the glass down. There was a dangerously long pause and she looked up, anticipating some sarcastic comment. But he shook his head as if he'd thought better of it and placed a tick alongside the figure.

Her sigh of relief came a little too soon.

'Doves? Are they in such demand too?' he enquired a few moments later, but politely, as if making an effort. He couldn't possibly be interested.

'I'm afraid so. And corn is not cheap,' she added, earning herself another of those long looks. She really needed to resist the snappy remarks. Especially as the gifts for the bridesmaids came next.

Candy had chosen bracelets for each of them from London's premier jeweller. No expense spared.

The nib of his pen hovered beside the item for a moment, then he said, 'Send them back.'

'What? No, wait.' He looked up. 'I can't do that!'

'You can't? Why not?'

Was he serious? Hadn't he taken the *slightest* interest in his own wedding?

'Because they're engraved with your names and the date.' This was cruel, she thought. One of his staff should be dealing with this. Pride was a killer... 'They were supposed to be a keepsake,' she added.

'Is that a fact?' Then, 'So? Where are they? These keepsakes.'

Could it get any worse? Oh, yes.

'Candy has them,' she admitted. 'She was having them gift-wrapped so that you could give them to the bridesmaids at the pre-wedding dinner.' He frowned. 'You *did* know about the pre-wedding dinner?'

'It was in my diary. As was the wedding,' he added. Caught by something in his voice, she looked up. For a moment she was trapped, held prisoner by his eyes, and it was all she could do to stop herself from reaching out to squeeze his hand. Tell him that it would get better.

As if he saw it coming, he gathered himself, putting himself mentally beyond reach.

She tried to speak and discovered that she had to clear her throat before she could continue.

'There are cufflinks for the ushers too,' she said, deciding it would be as well to get the whole jewellery thing over at once. 'And for you.'

'Were they engraved with our names too?'

'Just the date,' she replied.

'Useful in case I ever manage to forget it,' he said and, without warning, something happened to his mouth. She thought it might be a smile. Not much of one. Little more than a distortion of the lower lip, but Sylvie reached for the glass and took another sip of water.

It sizzled a little on her tongue, turning from ice-cold to lukewarm as it trickled down her throat. If he could do that with something so minimal, what on earth could he achieve when he was actually trying?

No. She didn't want to know. It didn't bear thinking about.

'I'm sure she'll return them,' she said in an effort to reassure him. Once she came back from wherever she was hiding out. She'd be eager to negotiate the sale of her story to whichever gossip magazine offered her the most to spill the beans on the break-up and the new man in her life before the story went cold.

Billionaireless, she would need the money.

'How sure?' he asked, holding the look for a full thirty seconds. 'And, even if she did, what would I do with them? Sell them on eBay?' She opened her mouth but, before she could speak, he said, 'Forget it.'

And, placing a tick against the item, he moved swiftly on.

It was only when they reached the cake that the cracks began to show in his icy self-control.

Candy, to her surprise, hadn't gone for some modern confection in white chocolate, or the witty little individual cakes that were suddenly all the fashion, but an honest-to-goodness traditional three-tier solid fruit cake, exquisitely iced by a master confectioner with the Harcourt coat of arms and Tom McFarlane's company logo in full colour on each layer.

The kind of cake where the top tier was traditionally put aside to be used as the christening cake for the first-born.

Until that point she'd almost felt as if Candy had been playing at weddings, more like a little girl let loose with the dressing-up box and her mother's make-up—or in this case a billionaire's bank account—than a woman embarking on the most important stage of her life. But that cake had suggested she'd been serious.

Maybe she'd just been trying to convince herself.

'Where is this monstrous confection?' Tom McFarlane asked.

'The cake?'

'Of course the damn cake!' he said, finally snapping, proving that he was made of more than stone. 'Did she take that with her too? Or has it already been foisted on some other unsuspecting male?'

'That's an outrageous thing to say, Mr McFarlane. The people I deal with are honest, hard-working businessmen and women.' She should have stopped then. 'Besides, no one wants a second-hand wedding cake.' Particularly one with someone else's coat of arms emblazoned on it.

'They don't? What a pity the same can't be said about brides.' For a moment she thought he was going to let it go. But not this time. 'So?' he demanded, glaring at her. 'What will happen to it?'

Desperate to get this over with, she was once more tempted to ask him if it mattered.

The words were on the tip of her tongue but then, for a split second, she caught a glimpse of the man beneath. A man who'd worked himself up from labouring in the markets to the top floor of a prestigious office building but had never forgotten how hard it had been or where he'd come from and was just plain horrified by such profligate waste and realised that, yes, to him it did matter.

'That's for you to decide,' she said.

'Then call the baker. He can deliver it to my apartment this evening.'

This was her cue to suggest that he was joking.

Had he any idea how big it was?

She restrained herself, but when she hesitated he sat back in his chair and gestured for her to get on with it.

'Do it now, Miss Smith.'

About to ask him what he'd do with ten pounds plus of the richest fruit cake—not including the almond paste and icing—she thought better of it. Maybe he liked fruit cake.

And when he got tired of it he could always feed the rest to the ducks.

It was all downhill from there with a mass of personalized stuff—all of it now just so much landfill. Menus, seating cards, table confetti in their entwined initials, candles, crackers with their names and the date on them, filled with little silver gifts for the guests—she'd managed to negotiate the return of the gifts. Every kind of personalized nonsense, each imprinted with their names and the date of the wedding that never was.

There wasn't a single thing that Candy had overlooked in her quest for the most extravagant, the most talked-about wedding of the season.

The list went on and on but the only other invoice to provoke a reaction was the one for the bon-bonnière.

'Well, here's something different,' he said, stretching for a touch of wry humour. 'A French tradition for wasting money instead of a British one.'

Seeing light at the end of the tunnel, she was prepared to risk a smile of her own but instead she caught her breath as, his guard momentarily down, she caught a glimpse of the grey hollows beneath his eyes, at his temple.

Maybe he heard because he looked up, a slight frown puckering his brow.

'What?' he demanded.

She shook her head, managed some kind of meaningless response that appeared to satisfy him, but after that she kept her head down and finally it was all done but for the last invoice. The one for her own fee, which she'd reduced by twenty per cent, even though the cancellation had caused nearly as much work as the actual day would have done.

'It's as well you don't offer a money back guarantee,' he said.

'My company's services carry a guarantee,' she assured him.

'But not one that covers parts replacement.'

Which was almost a joke but this time she didn't even think about smiling. 'I'm afraid not, Mr McFarlane. The bride is entirely your responsibility.'

'True,' he said, surprising her. 'But maybe you're missing out on a business opportunity,' he continued as, finally, he wrote the cheque. 'It would be so much simpler if one could pick and choose from a list of required qualities and place an order for the perfect wife.'

'Like a washing machine? Or a car?' she asked, wondering what, exactly, had been his specification for a wife. And whether he'd adjust it in the light of recent events.

Go for something less glamorous, more hard-wearing.

'Performance, style, finish…' She had been dangerously close to sarcasm but he appeared to take her analogy seriously. 'That sounds about right.' Then, as he tore the cheque from the book, 'But forget economy. Fast women and fast cars have that in common. They're both expensive to run. And you take a hit on the trade-in.' He didn't hand her the cheque but continued to look at it. 'Good business for you, though.'

'I'm not that cynical, Mr McFarlane,' she assured him as, refusing to sit there like a dummy while he made her wait for him to hand it over, she set about gathering her papers.

She tucked them back into the file and stowed them in her case, taking all the time in the world over it, just to prove that she was cool.

That nothing was further from her mind than a speedy exit from his office so that she could regain control over her breathing and her hormones, both of which had been doing their own thing ever since she'd been confronted at close quarters by whatever it was that Tom McFarlane had in such abundance. And she wasn't thinking about his money.

When everything was done she looked up and said, 'No one, no matter who they are, gets more than one SDS wedding.'

'Speaking personally, that's not going to be a problem.'

And he folded the cheque in two and tucked it into his shirt pocket.

No...

'Once has been more than enough.'

He stood up and hooked his jacket from the back of the chair before heading for the door.

No... Wait...

'Shall we go, Miss Smith?' he prompted, opening it, waiting for her.

'Go?' She stood up very slowly. 'Go where?'

'To pick up all this expensive but completely useless junk that I'm about to pay for.'

Oh. No. Really. That was just pointless. Besides the fact that she was now, seriously, running out of time as well as breath. Her staff didn't need her to hold their hands, but the pop diva was paying for that kind of service.

Sylvie was really annoyed with herself about that. Not the time—that was all down to Tom McFarlane. But the breath bit.

It wasn't even as if he'd *tried*. Done a single thing to account for her raised pulse rate or the pitifully twisted state of her hormones.

Apart from looking at her.

It was, apparently, enough.

'I'm qu-quite happy to dispose of it for you,' she said quickly. She could at least spare him the indignity of having to haul it to the recycling centre. Then, when that offer wasn't leapt on with grateful thanks, 'Or I can arrange to have it delivered.'

It wasn't as if he could be in a hurry for any of it.

'If that's more convenient for you,' he said. Her relief was short-lived. 'I assume you're not planning to charge me for storage?'

'Er, no…'

He nodded. 'I'm leaving the country tonight—my diary has been cleared, the honeymoon villa paid for—but I can hold on to the cheque until I get back next month and we can finish this then.'

What?

'I'll give you a call when I get back, shall I?'

Give her a call…?

Everyone had their snapping point. His had been the wedding cake. This was hers.

'You have got to be joking! I've already rearranged my afternoon for you and been kept waiting nearly an hour for my trouble. And I've got a party this evening.'

'Your social life is not my problem.'

'I don't have a social life!' she declared furiously.

'Really?' His glance was brief but all-encompassing, leaving her with the feeling that she'd been touched from head to foot in the most intimate way. And enjoying every moment of it.

Then he lifted one brow the merest fraction as if he knew…

'Really,' she snapped. Every waking moment of her life was spent making sure other people had a good time. 'This is business. And my van, unlike me, can't do two things at once.'

For some reason, that made him smile. And she'd been right about that too. Something about the way one corner of his mouth lifted, the skin crinkled around his eyes. The eyes heated…

'No problem,' he said, bringing her back to earth. 'For a reasonable fee, I'll hire your company one of mine.'

Beneath the riotous collage of balloons, streamers and showers of confetti with which Sylvie's van—the one presently engaged elsewhere—was painted, you could just about make out that its original colour was, like her mood, black.

Tom McFarlane's van was an identical model. Equally glossy and well cared for and equally black. In his case, however, the finish was unrelieved by anything more festive than his company's gold logo—TMF enclosed in a cartouche—so familiar from that wretched cake.

They'd ridden in his private lift down to the parking basement in total silence. With no choice but to go along with him, she was too angry to trust herself to attempt small talk.

Her sympathy was history. Sylvie no longer cared what he was feeling.

Smug self-satisfaction, no doubt, at putting her to the maximum possible inconvenience just because he could.

He led the way past an equally black and gleaming Aston Martin that was, no doubt, his personal transport. Fast and classy with voluptuous cream leather upholstery, it fitted his specification perfectly.

For a car or a wife.

Shame on Candy for dumping him; he *deserved* her!

They reached the van. He unlocked it, slid open the driver's door and held out the keys.

She stared at them.

She'd been tempted to insist on driving the van herself, if only to reclaim a little of the control which he'd wrested from her the moment she'd arrived at his office. If he was really serious about charging her for using it—and nothing about him so far suggested he had a sense of humour; his smile, when he'd finally let it go, had been pure wolf—it seemed eminently reasonable.

She'd had Tom McFarlane up to the eyebrows; he'd used up every particle of goodwill and she didn't want to spend one more minute with him than was absolutely necessary.

But she also wanted this over and done with as quickly as possible and had been counting on the fact that macho man wouldn't be able to stand by and watch her load and unload the thing by herself.

She might, of course, be fooling herself about that. It was quite possible he'd enjoy watching her work up a sweat as she earned every penny of her—reduced—fee. She was already regretting that twenty per cent. She'd earned every penny of it this afternoon.

Too late now. She'd just have to think of the eighty per cent she would be paid. The money for all those suppliers who'd put their heart and soul into making Candy's dream come true. And her reputation for being the kind of solid, dependable businesswoman whose word, in a business that was not short on flakes, meant something. Trust that had taken time to garner when her centuries-old name had, overnight, become a liability…

'I'd come and give you a hand but I have to take delivery of a cake.' Then, 'Do you need a hand up?'

'No, thanks,' she snapped back, snatching the keys from him

and tossing her bag on to the passenger seat. 'I've got one of these and I frequently drive it myself.'

'Not in that skirt or those heels, I'll bet.'

Oh, terrific!

That was where anger and speaking before your brain was engaged got you. But it was too late to change her mind because he didn't give her the chance to do so and back down gracefully. Instead he gave one of those I'm-sure-you-know-best shrugs—the ones that implied it was the last thing he thought—and stood back, leaving her to get on with it.

Unfortunately, getting on with it involved hoisting her narrow skirt up far enough to enable her to step up into the cab. Which was far enough for Tom McFarlane to get the full stocking tops and lace underwear experience.

The up side—there had to be an up side—was that it would be his breathing under attack for a change.

'Not that I'm complaining,' he assured her, apparently perfectly in control of his breathing.

And a good thing too, she decided. One of them ought to be in control of their bodily functions. Not that she bothered to dignify his remark with an answer, but let her skirt drop, smoothing it primly beneath her as she sat down, before placing the key in the ignition.

'What kept you?'

She'd had to buzz him so that he could let her through into the basement parking garage and by the time she'd pulled into the bay by the private lift that would take her directly to the penthouse loft apartment he was there, waiting for her.

His impatience touched a chord deep within her. Despite her very real, her *justifiable* anger with Tom McFarlane, her own impatience with every interruption, every traffic delay had been driven not by her need to be with an important client in Chelsea but by some blind, completely insane desire to get back to him. To renew the edgy, heat-filled connection.

He might make her angry but for the first time in years she felt like a woman and it was addictive…

'I can manage,' she assured him as he opened the door, offered her a helping hand. The default reaction of the modern woman. When did that happen?

It didn't matter; he took no notice. 'I've seen you manage once today. Since I've already seen your underwear, this time we'll do it my way.'

'A gentleman wouldn't have looked,' she gasped, outraged. *Outraged by the fact that he obviously thought her legs not worth a second look.*

'Is that a fact? I guess that just proves that I'm not a gentleman.' His eyes gleamed in the dim light of the underground garage. 'Didn't your old school chum tell you that it was one of the things she liked most about me? After my money. The risk. The realisation that for once in her life she wasn't in control.' He leaned close enough for her to feel his breath upon her cheek. For every cell to quiver with heightened awareness. Her skin to get goose-bumps. 'That she was playing with fire.'

Sylvie's mouth dried.

It worked for her.

'But then again,' he said, straightening, 'you're no lady, Miss Smith, or you'd have accepted my offer of assistance. So shall we try it again? Need a hand?'

'The only help I need is with the boxes,' she declared angrily. She certainly didn't need to hitch up her skirt to get down. All she had to do was swing her legs over the side and drop to the floor but, then again, Tom McFarlane was going out of his way to rile her, so why make it easy for him?

It wasn't as if she'd wanted to organise this wedding in the first place—especially not once she'd met the groom—but Candy had begged and when she wanted something, no one could deny her anything.

Except, it seemed, Tom McFarlane.

And maybe the house in Belgravia and the country estate were, after all, non-negotiable if you weren't marrying for love…

In retrospect, Sylvie thought, it was easy to see why she'd left so much of the detail to Quentin, but it really was too bad that, when all her instincts had been proved right, she was being punished by this man, not just for her bad judgement but for his too.

And her body seemed intent on joining in.

Maybe that was why, instead of jumping down, she put her hands flat against the seams of her skirt in a deliberately provocative manner, as a prelude to sliding it back up her legs.

To punish him—punish them both—right back.

Tom McFarlane couldn't believe the way he was behaving. He was already calling himself every kind of a fool. He'd cleared his desk in preparation for a month away and all he'd had to do was get on a plane. Instead, he'd demanded Sylvie Smith's presence in his office to explain her invoice. And then, as if that hadn't been sufficient misery for both of them, he'd made a complete fool himself by demanding she deliver a pile of useless junk to his apartment.

He'd already put himself through an afternoon of torment, looking at her long legs as she'd crossed and re-crossed them, her sexy high-heeled shoes highlighting the beauty of slender ankles.

They were the kind of legs that could give a man ideas—always assuming he hadn't got them the minute he'd set eyes on her. Hadn't had the best part of two hours, while she'd kept him waiting, to think about them.

But enough was enough and, before she could repeat the

move with the skirt, he snatched back control, seizing her around the waist to lift her down.

Taken by surprise, she gasped as she grabbed for his shoulders, bunching his shirt in her hands as she clung to him. She was not the only one short of breath. Close up, by the armful, Sylvie Smith's figure more than lived up to the promise glimpsed when she'd unbuttoned that sexy little jacket. All soft curves, it was the kind of figure that would look perfect in something soft and clinging. Would look even better out of it.

For a moment they were poised, locked together, just two people, holding each other, heat sizzling between them with only one thing on their minds—and it sure as hell wasn't wedding stationery.

A wisp of her streaky blonde hair brushed against his cheek and, as naturally as breathing, his hand slipped beneath the chocolate silk to cradle her ribcage, his thumb teasing the edge of a lace bra that he knew would exactly match the trim on what could only be French knickers.

There was no exclamation of outrage. Instead, as his thumb swept up over the aroused peak of her nipple, Sylvie Smith's lips parted, her breathing grew ragged and the look in her eyes was pure invitation as she seemed to melt against him, clinging to his shoulders as if they were the only thing keeping her on her feet.

It would be impossible to say whether it was the shudder that ran through her, her tongue moistening her hot, full lower lip or the tiny moan low in her throat that precipitated what happened next.

Or maybe it was none of those things. Maybe this had been in his mind from the very beginning, from the minute he'd first set eyes on her six months ago when he'd walked into her office and had instantly wanted to be anywhere else in the world.

Why he'd provoked today's meeting.

Because this raw, atavistic connection between two strangers, rather than a wedding that had lain like lead in his gut for weeks, was what today had been all about and the connection between them was as inevitable as it was explosive.

Control? Who did he think he was kidding…?

As his lips touched hers it was like oxygen to a fire that had been smouldering, unseen for months. One minute there was nothing. The next it was wildfire. Unstoppable…

Somehow they made it to the lift and he groped back for the key that closed the doors, sending it silently upward as they tore at the fastenings on each other's clothes, desperate for skin against skin. Just desperate.

A ping announced the arrival of an email from his office. Tom McFarlane bypassed the trip to Mustique, driven by a woman's tears to take the first long haul flight out with a vacant seat, and he'd hit the ground running the moment he'd touched down in the Far East. Work. Work had always been the answer.

He opened it. Read the note from his secretary and swore. Then he picked up the picture postcard of Sydney Opera House lying beside the laptop. Read the brief message—'Wish you were here'—not a question but a statement, before tearing it in two.

'I'll be fine…'

Famous last words, Sylvie thought as she regarded the pregnancy test. But then, when she'd said them, she hadn't been talking about the fact that she'd just had unprotected sex with a man with whom, despite the fact that he'd taken up residence in her brain, she'd never made it to first name terms.

She'd hoped, expected, that he'd call from Mustique, if only to make sure that there had been no consequences to their moment of madness. Maybe, even better, just to say hello. Best of all to say, I'd like to do that again…

Apparently he wouldn't. No doubt he thought that she'd have dealt with the possibility of any unforeseen consequences without a second thought. It was true; she had momentarily thought about emergency contraception while she'd been walking past a pharmacy the day after Tom McFarlane had made love to her. Then, just like some teenage kid buying his first packet of condoms, she'd come out with a new toothbrush.

Not because she was embarrassed, but because she had given it a second thought.

She was nearly thirty and a baby would not be bad news. She smiled as she lay her hand over her still perfectly flat abdomen. Far from it. It was wonderful news. Totally right. For her, anyway.

Quite what her baby's father would make of it was another matter altogether. She'd given up hoping for any kind of a call from him when she'd received a freshly drawn cheque in the post, clipped to a compliment slip with 'settlement in full' typed on it, followed by someone's indecipherable initials. Not his. Well, no, he was taking time out in the fabulous villa that Candy had chosen for their honeymoon.

He'd reinstated the twenty per cent she'd deducted and couldn't have made his point more succinctly. He'd known exactly what he was doing. Had regained control…

She returned the twenty per cent with a brief note, reminding him that she had deducted it from her bill. Stupid, no doubt, but pride had its price and it had been essential to make the point that she did not.

A secretary replied to thank her for pointing out the error, assuring her that Mr McFarlane had been informed.

She wasn't going to risk that this time. Or a formal letter from a lawyer demanding a paternity test. He had a right to know he was about to become a father, but she was going to make it plain that this was something he'd have to deal with himself and steeled herself to call his office.

She doubted that holidays came easily to him and fully expected that he would have returned early, but was informed that he was still away and did she want to leave a message?

She declined. A letter would be easier. That way she could keep it cool. She pulled a sheet of her personal notepaper from the rack, uncapped her pen.

An hour later she was still sitting there.

How did you tell a man you scarcely knew that he was about to become a father? Especially since Candy had shared her joy that ruining her figure to provide him with an heir had not been part of the deal.

How could she tell a man who apparently had no desire for children of his own that this was the most magical thing that had ever happened to her? Share just how amazing she felt, how happy she was? How life suddenly had real meaning?

She knew he'd hate that and, since she didn't want him angry, she'd keep it businesslike. Strictly to the point. Give him room to look past a moment of sizzling passion and see what they'd created together so that he could, maybe, find it in his heart to reach out to his child without any burden of liability to get in the way.

Finally, she began.

Dear Tom,

No. That wouldn't do. She blotted out the memory of crying his name out as he'd brought her body humming to life and scratched out *Tom* and, clinging instead to the memory of that twenty per cent, she wrote:

Dear Mr McFarlane—that was businesslike.

I'm writing to let you know that as a result of our recent...

She stopped again.

What? How could she put into words what had happened. His unexpected tenderness. The soaring joy that had brought the tears pouring down her face…

He hadn't understood the tears, how could he? She just kept saying, 'I'm all right…' Blissfully, brilliantly, wonderfully more than 'all right'. And she would have told him, but then Josie had rung in a panic because Delores was out of her head on an illegal substance half an hour before everyone was due to arrive and the baker had turned up with the cake and there had been no time. And all she'd said was, 'I have to go.'

She'd expected him to ring her. Kept hoping he would. But when she'd rung his office using the excuse of reminding him about the cheque—they'd somehow forgotten all about that—she'd been told he was away. He had, apparently, taken her at her word and caught his plane…

Come on, Sylvie. Get a grip. Keep it simple.

…as a result of our recent encounter, I am expecting a baby in July.

Businesslike. To the point. Cool. Except there was nothing cold about having a baby. When she'd seen the result of the pregnancy test there had been a rush of an emotion so powerful that she could hardly breathe…

Please believe me when I say that I do not hold you in any way responsible. It was my decision alone to go ahead with the pregnancy and I'm perfectly capable of supporting both myself and my son or daughter. My purpose in writing is not to make any demands on you, but obviously you have a right to know that you are about to become a father. Should you wish to be a part of his or her life, I would welcome your involvement without any expectation of commitment to me.

She crossed out *without any expectation of commitment to me.*
You could be too businesslike. Too cool…

*You have my assurance that I won't contact you again, or
ever raise the subject in the unlikely event that our paths
should cross. If I don't hear from you, I'll assume that you
have no wish to be involved.*
Yours
Sylvie Smith

What else could she say? That she would never forget him?
That he had broken down the protective wall that had been in place
ever since Jeremy had decided that he wasn't up for the 'worse'
or the unexpectedly 'poorer'—at least not with her—leaving her
with everything in place for a wedding except the groom.

That she would always be grateful to him for that. And for the
precious gift of a baby.

A new family. The chance to begin again…

No. That would be laying an emotional burden on him. Any
involvement must not be out of guilt, but because he wanted to
be a father. If he didn't, well, at least that way, her child would
be spared the bitter disillusionment she'd suffered at the hands
of her own father.

Something dropped on to the paper, puddling the ink. Stupid.
There was no reason for tears, absolutely none, and she palmed
them away, took out a fresh sheet of paper and wrote out her letter
minus the crossings out. Then she drove across to the other side
of the river and placed her letter in Tom McFarlane's letter box so
that she wasn't tempted to write again if he didn't reply, just in
case it had been lost in the post. Could be sure that no one else
would open it, read it…

Then, since there was nothing else to be done, she went home and started making plans for the changes that were about to happen in her life.

Tom managed to get the last seat on the flight back to London. Four months. He hadn't stopped travelling for four months. Like a man on the run, he'd been in flight from the memory, burned into his brain, of Sylvie Smith, silent tears pouring down her face.

For a moment, in that still, totally calm space, when he'd spilled his seed into her, he'd felt as if the entire world had suddenly been made over for him, that he was the hunter who'd come home with the biggest prize in the world.

Then he'd seen her tears and realised just what he'd done. That while she kept saying 'I'll be fine…' she was anything but. 'I have to go…' when all he wanted was to keep her close.

And work, he'd discovered, was not the answer, which was why he was going back to face her. To beg her to forgive him, beg her for more…

About to go through passport control, he paused at a book shop—with a twelve hour flight ahead of him, he'd need something to read—and found himself confronted by the face that haunted his dreams, both waking and sleeping. Not crying now, but smiling serenely out at him from the latest copy of *Celebrity.*

Saw the story flash—*'Sylvie's Happy Event!'*

He didn't need an interpreter to decipher 'happy event' and for a moment he felt a surge of something so powerful that he felt like a man with the world at his feet. She was wearing something soft and flowing and there was nothing to show that she was pregnant. Only the special glow of a woman who had just told the world that she was having a baby and was totally thrilled about it.

His baby…

He picked up the magazine. Opened it and came crashing back to earth as he saw that the cover photograph had been cropped. Inside, the same photograph showed that she was posed with a tall, fair-haired man and the caption read:

'Our favourite events organiser Sylvie Smith, who has just announced that she's expecting a baby later this summer, is pictured here with her childhood sweetheart, the recently divorced Earl of Melchester. Their marriage plans were put on hold when Sylvie's grandfather died and, as Jeremy put it, "life got in the way". It's wonderful to see them looking so happy to be together again and we confidently predict wedding bells very shortly.'

He read it twice, just to be sure, then he tossed the magazine in the nearest bin and went back to the desk to change his ticket.

'Where do you want to go, Mr McFarlane?'

'It doesn't matter.'

CHAPTER THREE

JOSIE FOWLER flung herself full length into the sofa that had, at considerable expense, been provided for the comfort of their clients. With her feet dangling over the arm and her arm shielding her eyes, she groaned.

'Late night?' Sylvie asked.

'Late and then some. I have to tell you that you are, without doubt, a world class fantasy wedding planner.'

'*Event* planner,' Sylvie said, pulling a face. She was so *off* weddings. 'We are SDS *Events,* Jo. Fantasy or otherwise, weddings are no different from any other job.' *Cue, hollow laughter…* 'I take it from your reaction that everything went according to plan yesterday?'

In other words, please tell me that the bride didn't have second thoughts…

'Pleease!' Josie, in full drama queen mode—despite her eighteen-hole Doc Martens and punk hair-do, both of them purple—clutched both hands to her heart. 'What SDS *event* would dare to deviate from "the plan"?'

'According to my grandfather,' she said in an effort not to think about the Harcourt/McFarlane debacle—she'd promised herself she wouldn't think about that nightmare, or the Tom

McFarlane effect, more than three times a day and she was already over budget— 'the first casualty of battle is always "the plan".'

She laid her hand over the child growing beneath her heart— living proof of that little homily.

'That would be your Colonel-in-Chief of the regiment grandfather, right?'

'It certainly wasn't my party-throwing playboy grandfather. His idea of "a plan" was to order enough champagne to float a battleship and leave everything else for someone else to worry about.' Including the final bill. And the sweetest man on earth. 'As you'll learn, when emotions are involved anything can happen,' she continued as, letter in hand, she carefully placed a tick on one of the plans that decorated every available inch of wall space.

This one was for a silver wedding celebration. She felt safe with a silver wedding. Then, hand on her back, she straightened carefully.

'Are you okay?' Josie asked. Then, 'Sit down, I can do that.'

'It's done,' she said, waving away her concern. 'Don't fuss.' Then, 'Tell me about the wedding.'

'I *have* told you. It was fabulous.' Then, 'You're not *still* smarting over the bride who got away, are you?'

'No!' Her legendary calm slipped a notch and not just because of the wedding that never was. 'No,' she repeated, getting a grip. 'The one thing I can't be held responsible for is the bride getting cold feet. Even if she chose to warm them on one of my staff.'

'You are not responsible! For heaven's sake, it was more than six months ago. Even the groom will have got over it by now.'

'I couldn't say.' All she knew was that he hadn't responded to her letter. 'Can we please just concentrate on yesterday's wedding?' she said, jerking her mind away from that long afternoon she'd spent with Tom McFarlane. The solidity of his shoulders beneath her hands. The way his hands had felt against her skin. That raw, overwhelming need as he'd looked down at her, touched her…

The only thing on his mind had been instant gratification with the first woman to cross his path. It had been nothing more than a reaction to being dumped, she knew. A wholly masculine need to have his ego restored. With maybe a little tit-for-tat payback thrown in for good measure. Just in case she needed to feel any worse about herself.

'Look, if you don't trust me, Sylvie, maybe you should find someone—'

Jerked back from the danger of slipping into self-pity, she said, 'Oh, Josie… Of course I trust you! I wouldn't leave such a major event to anyone in whom I didn't have the utmost faith. Besides, I knew you'd rather be coordinating a wedding in the Cotswolds than babysitting a women's rights conference in London. Sensible woman that you are.' Then, with determined brightness, 'So, not a single hiccup, then? There'll be no comebacks when I send the bride's papa the final account?'

'Anyone who didn't know you better, Sylvie, would think you only cared about the money.'

'I promise you, I don't do this for fun,' she replied.

'Oh, right. As if you didn't work yourself to a standstill to ensure that every little detail was perfect so that the bride has a day she'll never forget.'

'That's just good business, Jo. I apply exactly the same standards to every event.'

'You're a perfectionist, no doubt about it. But you do always seem to go the extra mile for weddings.'

'I just worry more. It's not quite like a conference or some company event, is it? For the two people involved it's a once in a lifetime occasion. If it goes wrong they aren't going to say, "Oh, well, never mind. We'll have the fireworks next time." At least I hope not!'

'I knew it! You're just like the rest of us. Beneath that ice-cool exterior beats a heart of pure mush.'

'Rubbish. Mush, let me tell you, doesn't pay the bills,' she said crisply. It certainly hadn't been 'mush' she'd felt...

No. She was overdrawn on thinking about Tom McFarlane. Overdrawn and heading for bankruptcy.

'So?' she continued a touch desperately. 'Did we do good?'

'We did great,' Josie said, lowering her feet to the floor and joining her at the wall plan. 'It was perfection from the moment the bride arrived in her fairy tale coach until the last firework faded in the midnight sky.' She sighed. 'You were absolutely right, by the way, to resist the bride's plea for bows on the tails of the horses.'

'You didn't say that when she had hysterics in the office,' Sylvie reminded her. 'As I recall, your exact words were, "Give the silly cow what she wants..."'

'I just don't have your class, Sylvie.'

'It's easy to get carried away.' To lose sight of what a wedding actually meant in the pressure to indulge in every over-the-top frill. 'When in doubt just think of it as a feathers-and-curls situation. If you have feathers in your hat, who's going to notice the curls?'

'You see? I would go for both every time. I guess that's the difference between Benenden and a sink estate comprehensive school...'

'Not necessarily.'

It certainly hadn't stopped Candy Harcourt from going for the feathers, the curls and every other frippery known to woman-kind. But then she'd had a big empty gap to fill, one that had taken all the frippery she could get her hands on, and it still hadn't been enough.

When it had been the real thing, Candy had only needed the man she loved and a couple of witnesses. Of course that might have been because his family would have done everything they could to stop it if they'd had advance warning.

They'd sent her a photograph that someone had taken of them after the ceremony, along with a note from Candy apologising for leaving her to deal with the fallout and one from Quentin tendering his resignation.

It had been plain that he was hoping that she'd beg him to come back but she'd managed to resist the temptation and, to her relief, he'd already been snapped up by one of her competitors.

'Besides,' she said, doing her utmost to banish Candy and Quentin and their somewhat unexpected happy ever after from her memory, 'you have the street smarts, Jo. One look from you and everyone thinks twice about giving us the run-around.'

Tom McFarlane wouldn't have given Josie a moment's trouble, she thought.

'And no one is better at keeping everything running behind the scenes on the big day,' she continued. 'Taking you on was the best day's work I ever did.'

Which was, despite the many warnings she'd received to the contrary, absolutely true.

Josie looked at her, swallowed and muttered, 'Thanks.' And, in an attempt to cover her confusion, bent to see what she'd been doing. 'Hey, you've found another piper!'

'Let's hope this one doesn't take a notion to do a spot of mountaineering and break something vital before the big day.' She stood back. 'Now all I need is for the happy couple to finalise the menu and, since the Rolling Stones are a little out of the budget for this affair, an RS tribute band so that the guests can revisit their ill-spent youth in a night of rock and roll.' Then, 'Did those new caterers do the business?'

'For goodness' sake, Sylvie! I told you it was perfect!'

'There's no such thing as perfect,' she said, but with a smile. 'Just find me some little thing and I'll stop worrying.'

'Idiot.' Then, 'Okay, the horses pooped in front of the church, hence my change of heart about the ribbons. Will that do?'

'That is perfect,' she said. Sylvie knew it was stupid, but there was always *something;* it was like waiting for the other shoe to drop. 'You made sure it was cleaned up?'

Josie grinned. 'I got lucky. The church warden was hoping for a donation for his roses and he was all ready with a bucket and shovel.'

'You both got lucky, then.'

'Too right. And, to put your mind totally at rest, the flowers were out of this world,' Josie said, holding up her hand and ticking the items off one by one. 'The choir were angelic. The food was amazing, those caterers are definitely a find. The string quartet, as far as I could tell—that is *soooo* not my kind of music—played in tune. Even the sun shone.' Having run out of fingers, she shrugged. 'What else is there?'

'You want a list?' Sylvie held up her own hand, ready to tick off the five legendary worst ever wedding disasters that every planner dreaded. Apart from the bride changing her mind days before the wedding.

Or the wedding planner losing it with the forsaken groom, she thought, forgetting the list as she placed her hand on the growing bulk of the baby she was carrying.

That was an item of gossip that would have made the *story* into a *STORY* and she came out in a cold sweat just thinking about what a meal *Celebrity* would make of it if they ever found out whose baby she was carrying.

Not that they hadn't tried. Jeremy had been less than amused to be lined up as a possibility and had called her demanding she deny the rumours.

It was cruel not to, and maybe if he hadn't behaved like such a pompous ass she'd have done it. Not that he'd actually changed, she realised. She was the one who'd done that, but only after wasting ten years…

'The list?' Josie prompted, looking at her a little oddly. She might not have believed the official version, that the single mother pregnancy had been planned using a 'donor'. She hadn't elaborated and Josie hadn't pushed it. And, rising thirty with no partner and a ticking biological clock, even her closest friends had let it go without more than a slightly raised eyebrow.

'Oh, right, the list…'

Before she could begin, the phone rang.

She reached back, glanced at the caller ID and, picking it up, said, 'Hi, Laura. How are you?'

'Pretty good, thanks, Sylvie, but, as always, I'm in need of a favour.'

'Let me guess. You want an "SDS Event" for the silent auction at this year's Pink Ribbon Club lunch?'

'No…' Then, 'Well, yes, obviously, if you're offering. We raised a bundle on that last year.'

'Then it's yours.'

'That's very generous. Thank you. I'll just write that in…' She paused, presumably to make a note of it.

'So?' Sylvie prompted. 'What's the favour?'

'Oh, yes! It is a big one, although on this occasion I'm in a position to offer you something in return for your efforts.'

'Oh?' Laura sounded really excited but not missing the fact that she would be making an 'effort', Sylvie sat down and, pulling her notebook towards her, said, 'Okay, let's hear it.'

'You're not going to believe this, but I've just had a phone call from *Celebrity* magazine. They want to do a feature on the charity and they're using the Spring Wedding Fayre we're holding as a backdrop. They've even offered us a generous donation for our co-operation.'

'They have?' No wonder she was excited. 'They usually only pay for exclusive coverage,' she warned. 'That won't win you any friends with the local press. Willow Armstrong has been very supportive.'

'I know, but this won't affect local coverage. *Celebrity* are prepared to be generous because we're pulling out all the stops for the Club's tenth anniversary. That's why I approached them in the first place. Your mother was always one of their favourites. All those wonderful parties…'

'Yes…'

Throwing parties was something of a family tradition. Experience she'd put to profitable use when everything had gone belly-up.

'So what do you want from me?'

'Well, your mother founded the charity…'

'Yes.'

'And you are our Honorary President.'

Laura's slow build-up was beginning to make her uneasy. 'And?'

'Well, it all just fits together so perfectly, don't you see? Your mother's parties. And now you're the wedding planner at the top of every bride's wish list.'

'Event planner, Laura. Weddings are just one part of our business.'

'I know, I know, but honestly they've come up with the most brilliant idea. One that I know you're going to love.'

'Really?'

When it came to some 'brilliant idea' concocted by the features editor of a gossip magazine, 'love' was unlikely to be her first reaction but Sylvie reserved judgement until she heard what it was.

'Really. They're going to feature a fantasy wedding, using our exhibitors. That's going to be their exclusive.'

'Oh, I see…' Actually that *was* a good idea… 'Well, well done, you.' Then, 'You want me to give you some ideas for the fantasy thing, is that it? I'll be happy to—'

'No, Sylvie, I want a little bit more than that.' Laura could scarcely contain herself. 'A lot more than that, actually. What they want is for you to use the Fayre's exhibitors to create your *own* fantasy wedding!'

'Mine? But I'm not getting married.'

Laura gave a little tut as if she were being particularly dim. 'No, no, no… Don't you see? You've organised so many fabulous weddings for other people that everyone will be agog to know what you'd choose for yourself.'

Oh, confetti!

The *Celebrity* features editor must have spotted her name on the letterhead and thought all her birthdays had come at once.

'Bride, groom, two witnesses and the local register office?' she offered hopefully.

Laura laughed, confident she was being teased. 'I think *Celebrity* will want something a little more fairy tale than that!'

Oh, yes. *Celebrity* would want everything, up to and including her heart on her sleeve, which they were apparently ready to extract with a blunt knife. They couldn't have been more obvious.

'Just think what fun it will be,' Laura continued. 'Gorgeous clothes, fabulous food, all those special touches you're so famous for. We've got some truly wonderful local exhibitors and you can totally let yourself go—'

'Laura,' she said, cutting in before this went any further. 'I'm sorry, really, but I can't do that.'

There was a moment of stunned silence. Then Laura, stiff now, said, 'I realise that there won't be any big London names, Sylvie, but there's no need to be quite that dismissive.'

Oh, good grief, she'd misunderstood. It wasn't the exhibitors she was turning down. It was the whole nightmare scenario.

'No…' she began, but it was too late.

'Your mother, if she were still with us—'

Sylvie lowered her head into her hand, knowing what was coming and helpless to stop it.

'Lady Annika would be very disappointed to think that you'd let us down.'

No! No! No! Sylvie stuffed her fist into her mouth to stop the scream leaking out.

Josie, staring at her, mouthed the word, 'Trouble?'

She just shook her head, unable to answer. This wasn't trouble; this was the old girl network in full working order and, if nothing else would do it, the 'old girls' would play the guilt card without a second's thought.

'You may be an important businesswoman these days, but people still remember your family. Remember you. You're a local girl and you have a duty to fly the flag for your town.' As if aware that her attention was drifting, Laura pitched her voice at a level capable of cutting cold steel. 'Forget your mother's charity…' *oh, low blow!* '…these people should be able to count on your support.'

The guilt card swiftly followed by the demands of *noblesse oblige.* Because, even when the *noblesse* had gone well and truly down the pan, the *oblige* just refused to quit.

Guilt and duty. The double whammy.

'This feature wouldn't just be fabulous PR for you, it would give some small designers a real chance to get noticed—'

Okay! Enough!

There was no need to lay it on with a trowel. Once the 'your mother would be disappointed' gambit had been played, Sylvie knew it was all over bar the shouting and, pulling herself together, she attempted to stem the flow.

'Laura…'

'Of course I don't suppose *you* need PR these days—'

'*Laura!*'

'And, as for the fee *Celebrity* are offering the charity, well—'

'Laura, don't you ever read *Celebrity?*'

'Well, no. It's not my kind of thing. You won't tell them, will you?'

'No, but that's not the point. If you ever read the thing, you'd know that the reason I can't possibly do this is because I'm six months pregnant.'

'Pregnant?' Then, 'I didn't realise. When did you get married?'

Sylvie added 'hurt' to the range of expressions in Laura's voice.

'I didn't, Laura. I'm not.'

'Oh, *well,* that's even better. You can really—'

'No,' she said quickly, anticipating what was coming next. 'I can't. I'm not getting married.' Could this get any worse? 'I just wanted a baby.'

Or better.

Because it was true.

Once she'd got over the shock, she'd realised that she did want this little girl. Desperately.

Laura, momentarily stumped, quickly recovered. 'Oh, well, it doesn't actually matter, does it? You don't have to appear in the feature. No one would expect you to actually model something you'd chosen for yourself. Not before the wedding. Bad luck and all that? I'm sure *Celebrity* can organise a lookalike model.'

'Do they have to? Couldn't they find someone a little taller, a little thinner,' she said, making a joke of it. Trying not to think what Tom McFarlane would make of it.

She'd expected him to call her. What she expected him to say, she didn't dare think about. But she'd given him the option to walk away and he'd apparently taken it.

'How much are *Celebrity* offering?' she asked, refusing to dwell on it. Ignoring the hurt. And, certain that she'd won, Laura gave her the figure.

For a clutching-at-straws moment she'd hoped she might be able to cover the sum herself, buy her freedom. But, even as she'd clutched, she'd known that it was never going to happen.

This was about more than money.

It was about raising the profile of the charity that her mother had founded. A chance to show a national audience what they'd achieved, maybe even encourage women to set up branches in other areas; charities, like every other organization, had to grow or die. About giving local artists and craftsmen a national stage on which to air their talent.

And it was for her too. Refusing to hide.

Settled in her mind, Sylvie drew a deep breath and, burning all her boats, said, 'Actually, Laura, that's not enough.'

'What isn't enough?'

'The fee *Celebrity* are offering you. It isn't enough.'

'It isn't?' Laura asked, surprised out of her disapproval as she was thrown on the defensive. 'I thought it was very generous.'

'I'm sure they told you that, but for this feature…' for Sylvie Duchamp Smith giving a wedding master-class, for another excuse to rake over old bridal coals and speculate on the identity of the father of her child '…they'll pay twice that.'

'No!'

'Oh, yes!' The magazine had picked up the tabs for a couple of the weddings she'd organised and she knew what she was talking about. If they wanted to fill their pages with her personal fantasy, the charity her mother had founded was going to be paid the going rate. 'You can take my word for it.'

'Oh, I do,' Laura assured her, suddenly catching on to the fact that she'd hooked her fish. 'Maybe, as our Honorary President, you could talk to them? Since you seem to know so much about it.'

She fought down the temptation to remind the charity's Chairman that the post of 'Hon Pres' was supposed to be just that, an honorary one, and said, 'Leave it to me.' She could, if nothing else, use the opportunity to ensure that the features editor focused on the fantasy wedding and, for her full co-operation, leave old stories buried. 'So where is this all going to take place?'

'I've been saving the best until last,' she said. 'We've been offered the use of Longbourne Court for the Fayre. Back where it all began.'

Longbourne Court.

Sylvie, expected to respond enthusiastically, discovered that her tongue was refusing to connect with the roof of her mouth.

'Isn't that just perfect?' Laura said when Sylvia failed to say it for her.

There was no such thing as perfect…

A slightly flat, 'Great,' was the best she could manage.

'It was bought several months ago by some billionaire busi-nessman and we've all been agog, as you can imagine.'

Oh, yes, she could imagine. It would have been the talk of coffee mornings and bridge parties across the county.

'Obviously, we all hoped he was going to live in it, but he's instructed Mark Hilliard, the architect…?' She paused, waiting for her to acknowledge the name.

'Mmm…'

'He's instructed Mark to draw up plans to convert the house into a conference centre.'

'Oh?'

'It's a shame, of course,' she said, finally cottoning on to a lack of enthusiasm from her audience. 'It's such a beautiful house. But there you are.'

Yes, indeed, there she was.

'Since it's "listed" it's going to take a while to sort out, but the *Celebrity* feature will give it one last outing and it's fitting that its swansong will honour your mother. And that you'll be part of it.'

'I hope the planning people won't be too difficult,' she said, without commenting on the fittingness or not of her participation in its final moments as a country house. 'Longbourne has been empty for much too long.'

The rock star who'd bought it originally hadn't spent more than a weekend or two there and since he'd fallen from the balcony of his New York penthouse, leaving his affairs in a mess, several years ago there had been nothing but gossip and rumour about what would happen to the estate.

Not that she'd been listening. That was all in the past. History.

'Well, whatever is planned isn't going to happen until English Heritage have had their say on the subject,' Laura said. 'That's how I heard what was happening; George is on the local committee, you know. That's when it occurred to me that in the meantime our billionaire might like the opportunity to demonstrate his credentials as a good neighbour.'

'And he agreed?'

'I suppose so. I actually spoke to some woman who appears to be in charge of the day-to-day running of the company and she was really enthusiastic about helping the charity. Well, everyone has been touched, haven't they?'

Woman at the helm or not, she doubted that sentimentality had much to do with the decision.

'The fact that the proposed conference centre will get acres of free publicity in *Celebrity* wouldn't have anything to do with that, I suppose?'

'Oh, Sylvie! Don't be so cynical.'

Why, just because she had a reputation for planning fantasy parties and weddings, did everyone think she should be sentimental? It was just *business*…

'And even if his company does get something out of it, well, what of it? I know it was your home, Sylvie, but times have changed and the conference centre will provide jobs locally. It's a win-win-win situation.'

'I suppose so.' Sylvie had made a point of staying well clear of her family home since it had been sold lock, stock and barrel, to pay off her grandfather's creditors, but Laura was right. The publicity would be good for everyone.

The Pink Ribbon Club charity founded by her mother; local designers; the tradesmen who would be employed to work on the conversion as well as local businesses.

In fact, when it came right down to it, the entire Melchester economy apparently rested on what frock she'd choose to wear to her own fantasy wedding.

Fantasy being the operative word. One fantasy in a lifetime was enough and she hadn't been kidding about the register office.

But, with Longbourne Court in the equation, *Celebrity* was going to have to stump up vastly more than their original offer. This was big and if they wanted to make themselves look good by clinging on to the trailing pink ribbons of her mother's charity, they were going to have to pay for the privilege.

Tom McFarlane drew up in front of the tall wrought iron gates of Longbourne Court.

Two things were wrong.

They were standing wide open.

And, decorating each of the central finials, was a large knot of pink ribbons.

He picked up his cellphone and hit fast dial.

'Tom?' Unsurprisingly, his CEO was surprised to hear from him. 'Isn't it the middle of the night where you are?'

'Right at this moment I'm at the gates of Longbourne Court, Pam, and I'm looking at pink ribbons. Please tell me that I'm hallucinating.'

'You're back in the UK?' she responded, ignoring his plea. Then, 'At Longbourne?'

A long blast on an air horn drowned out his reply, which was probably just as well.

'I'm sorry if I've returned in time to spoil the party,' he said, not stinting on the sarcasm, 'but I've got pink ribbons in front of me and an irate trucker with his radiator an inch from my rear. Just tell me what the hell is going on.'

'Hi, Pam,' she prompted, ignoring his question. 'I'm sorry I'm being a grouch but I'm jet lagged. As soon as I've had a decent night's sleep I'll hand over the duty-frees, along with the big fat bonus I owe you for taking care of—'

'I'm not in the mood,' he warned.

'No? Well, it's a lovely day and maybe by the time you reach the house you'll have remembered where you mislaid your manners,' she replied, completely unperturbed. 'When you do, you'll find me in the library running your company.'

'You're here?' he demanded. Stupid question. Pink ribbons and trucks didn't appear without someone to organise them. Pam obviously thought so too, since her only response was the dialling tone.

The truck driver sounded off for the second time and, resisting the temptation to swear at the man—he was only trying to do his job, whatever that was—he tossed the phone on the seat beside him and drove through the gates.

The trees were breaking out in new leaf and the parkland surrounding Longbourne Court had the timeless look of a set for some boobs-and-breeches costume drama, an illusion rudely shattered as he crested the rise.

The house was standing golden and square in the bright sunshine, just as it had for the best part of three centuries, but the only horsepower on show was of the twenty-first century variety. Trucks, cars, vans.

The nearest belonged to a confectioner who, according to the signage on her faux vintage vehicle, proclaimed to the world in copperplate script that she specialized in bespoke wedding cakes. One glance confirmed that there were caterers, photographers, florists—in fact, anything you could think of—ditto.

The kind of scene he'd so narrowly avoided six months ago, when Candy had decided that mere money wasn't enough to compensate for his lack of breeding and had traded up to a title. Not that 'Hon' was that big a deal but if she hung in there she'd make it to Lady eventually.

She could, with advantage, have taken lessons from her good friend Sylvie Smith. She hadn't messed about, she'd gone straight for the big one; she'd made damn sure that the 'childhood sweetheart', the one who'd make her a countess, didn't get away a second time.

CHAPTER FOUR

Tom parked his Aston in the coach house, alongside Pam's zippy BMW coupé and a black and silver Mini that he didn't recognise, but which presumably belonged to one of her staff. Inside the house it was all noise and chaos as the owners of the vehicles milled about, apparently in the process of setting up shop in his house.

He didn't pause to enquire what the devil they thought they were doing, instead hunting down the person responsible. The woman he'd left to keep his company ticking over while he put as much distance between himself and London as possible.

He found her sitting behind an antique desk in the library, looking for all the world like the lady of the manor.

'What the hell is going on?' he asked.

She peered over the top of her spectacles. 'Nice tan,' she said. 'Shame about the manners.'

'Pink ribbons,' he countered, refusing to be diverted.

'Maybe coffee would help. Or would you prefer tea? Better make it camomile.'

He placed his hands on the desk, leaned forward and, when he was within six inches of her face, he said, 'Tell me about the ribbons, Pam.'

'You are supposed to grovel, you wretch,' she said. 'Six

months! You've been away six months! I had to cancel my trip to South Africa and I've totally missed the skiing season—'

'What's to miss about breaking something vital?'

She almost smiled.

'Come on, Pam, you're the one who made the point that the honeymoon was booked so I might as well give myself a break.'

'What I had in mind was a couple of weeks chilling out on a beach. Or raising hell if that's what it took. As I recall, you weren't that keen.'

'I wasn't and I didn't. When I got to the airport I traded in my ticket for the first flight out.'

'And didn't tell a soul where you were. You did a six-month disappearing act!'

'I wish. You can't hide from email.'

She shrugged. 'I kept it to the minimum.'

'You're not fooling me, Pam Baxter. You've had absolute control while I've been away and you've loved every minute of it.'

'That's not the point! Have you any idea how worried I've been?' Then, presumably to distract him from the fact that she'd backed down before he'd apologised, she said, 'And, as for the ribbons on the gate, I don't know anything about them. But if I had to make a guess I'd suggest that the Pink Ribbon Club put them there.'

Okay.

He was distracted.

'What the hell is the Pink Ribbon Club when it's at home?' he asked, but easing back. He'd known she'd worry, but hanging around to offer explanations hadn't been appealing. 'And, more to the point, why are they hanging the damn things from my gate?'

She offered him a brochure from a stack on the desk. 'I've given them permission to hold a Wedding Fayre here—that's

Fayre with a y and an e—so I imagine they're advertising the fact to passing traffic. That's why I'm here this week,' she explained. 'The couple who are caretakers of the place do a good job, but I can't expect them to be responsible for the house and its contents with so many people coming and going.'

'Why?' he asked.

'Why did I give the PRC permission to stage the Fayre here? It's a local charity,' she said. 'Founded by Lady Annika Duchamp Smith?'

He stared at the wedding bell and horseshoe bedecked brochure for a moment before dropping it and subsiding into an ancient leather armchair.

'The Duchamp family owned the house for generations,' she prompted when he didn't respond. 'It's their coat of arms on the gate.'

'Really. Well, that covers the Duchamps. What's the story on the Smiths?' he asked, remembering a Smith with that hallmark English aristocratic cool and a voice that told the world everything they needed to know about her class, background.

A Smith with silvery-blue eyes that not only looked as if they could cause chaos if they had a mind to, but had gone ahead and done it.

Pam shrugged. 'Presumably Lady Annika married a Mr Smith.'

'For his money rather than his name, apparently, since she chose not to relinquish her own.'

For a moment there, when the word *charity* had been invoked, he'd found himself on the back foot but he quickly rallied. These people stood for everything he loathed.

Privilege, inherited wealth, a belief in their own innate superiority.

People for whom charity meant nothing more than another social event.

For a while he'd been dazzled too. Then completely blinded. But he had both feet firmly back on the ground now.

'It'll take more than playing charity queen to get Lady Annika back inside Longbourne Court,' he said.

'Well, actually Lady Annika—'

'I mean it,' he cut in, not interested in her ladyship. 'Give the Ribbon mob a donation if you think they're doing a good job, but get rid of her. And her Fayre with a y and an e.' He snorted with disgust. 'Why do they spell it like that?'

'Beats me,' she replied, 'but I'm afraid you're stuck with it. Even if it wasn't far too late to ungive permission, I wouldn't. *Celebrity* magazine are covering the event—which is why we need a dress rehearsal so that they can get photographs. Your conference centre is about to get the kind of publicity that money just can't buy.'

'You didn't know I was planning a conference centre.'

'Oh, please! What else are you going to do with it? Live here? On your own? Besides, our favourite architect, Mark Hilliard, sent me a sheaf of forms from the Planning Department.'

'He didn't waste any time!' Then, realising that Pam was looking at him a little oddly, 'Which is good. I stressed the need to get on with it when I spoke to him.'

'Oh? You managed to find time to *speak* to your architect.'

'It was a matter of priorities. The sooner we get started on this, the better.'

'In that case, the publicity is good news.'

'You think? This may come as a surprise to you, Pam, but the people—the *women*—who read gossip magazines, who go to Wedding Fayres, spelled with a y and an e, do not organise conferences.'

'I arrange conferences,' she pointed out.

'You are different.'

'Of course I'm not. And I never miss an edition of *Celebrity*.'

'You're kidding?'

'Am I?' She didn't bother to reassure him, just said, 'You're nothing but an old-fashioned misogynist at heart, aren't you, Tom?'

'You can't get around me with compliments—'

'And maybe the teeniest bit of a snob?'

'A snob!' On the contrary, he was the self-made man whose bride-to-be had decided that, once spending his money— egged on by her old school chum, Miss Smith—had lost its novelty, and the mists of lust had cleared, he wasn't good enough to marry.

'An inverted one,' she elaborated, as if that was any better.

'I'm a realist, Pam.'

'Oh, right, that would be the realist who fell off the edge of the earth six months ago, leaving me to hold the fort?'

'Which disproves your misogynist theory. If I disliked women, why would I leave you in charge while I took some much needed time out? Unlike you, I don't take three holidays a year. And why would I have appointed you as my CEO in the first place? Besides, I kept in touch.'

'Because I'm damn good at my job,' she said, answering the first two parts of his question. 'But, for your information, the occasional email to keep me up to date with the real estate you've been vacuuming up on whichever continent you happened to be at the time so that I could deal with the paperwork, is not keeping in touch.'

'I'm sure I sent you a postcard from Rio,' he said. The only one he really remembered was the one he hadn't sent.

'"Wish you were here"? Chance would have been a fine thing. Besides, I wanted to know how you were.' Then, 'You've lost weight.'

'I'm fine, okay!' She didn't look convinced. 'Truly. But I

decided that since I was taking a break I might usefully expand my empire while I was about it.'

'That's not expanding your empire, it's called displacement activity,' Pam said, giving him what his grandmother would have described as an old-fashioned look. 'If you were a woman, you'd have bought shoes.'

'Which proves my point about women,' he said. 'Real estate is a much better investment.'

'And, assuming you were thinking at all, which I take leave to doubt,' Pam continued, ignoring that and returning to the third part of his question, 'I'd suggest it's because you don't think of me as a woman at all.'

'Which is the highest compliment I could pay you.'

'Is that right? And you're surprised that Candy Harcourt dumped you?'

Surprised was not actually the first word that had come to mind. Relieved… Evading the question, he said, 'So, is this Wedding Fayre your idea of payback for leaving you to do your job?'

'Well, if I'd known you were going to be here, that would definitely have been a bonus. As it is, like you, I was being realistic. This is business. I *am* doing my job. Looking after your interests in your absence.' She gave him a long, hard look. 'And, as my last word on that subject, I suggest you go down on your knees and thank Candida Harcourt—or should I say The Honourable Mrs Quentin Turner Lyall—for letting you off the hook.'

'She actually married him?'

'It's true love, according to *Celebrity.*' Then, when he scowled at the mention of the magazine, 'Be grateful,' she said, misunderstanding his reaction. 'Divorce would have cost you a lot more than the fancy wedding she ran out on.'

'Thanks for the vote of confidence.' He dragged his hair back from his forehead. It immediately flopped over his forehead again. It needed cutting…

'It's not you that I doubt.' She shrugged. 'Impoverished aristocracy are always a risk. Marrying for money goes with the territory. In the old days they had no choice but to stick with the deal, but these days divorce is just as profitable. Not that I'm suggesting your only attraction was fiscal.'

'In other words, she was just amusing herself with a bit of rough? Got carried away for a moment…'

Something else she had in common with her old school chum, Sylvie Smith. No wonder she'd cried. He'd only lost Candy while her indiscretion could have lost her the ermine and the guaranteed seat at the next coronation…

Pam raised her hands in a gesture that could have meant anything but, taking the opportunity to change the subject, he indicated the noises off in the entrance hall.

'I appear to have no choice but to accept that this is a done deal. How long is it going to last?'

'The Fayre? It'll all be over by Monday.'

'A week? I've got to put up with pink ribbons on my gates for a week?' he demanded.

'Be glad this isn't Italy—everyone would be congratulating you on the birth of a daughter.'

'That's not remotely funny,' he declared. Anything but.

'For heaven's sake, Tom, lighten up.' Then, more gently, 'If you'd given me some indication that you were coming home I'd have warned you what was happening. Why don't you go back to London? Catch up with everyone. Longbourne Court will still be here next week.'

'Nice idea, but I've arranged to meet Mark Hilliard here this morning.'

'I could put him off until next week.'

'No,' he said, hauling himself out of the chair and heading for the door. 'I want to get started.' He wanted to subject the house to his will; making it entirely his would draw a line under the whole affair. 'Give me twenty minutes to take a shower and you can bring me up to date. There is hot water, I take it?'

'Plenty. I'll get Mrs Kennedy to make up the bed in the master suite.'

'Thanks. And if you were serious about the coffee, that would be good too.'

'I'll get on to it.' Then, as he opened the door, she called, 'Oh, Tom! Wait! Before you go, I should warn you—'

'Twenty minutes,' he repeated, closing it behind him, then stood back as two men manhandled a large sheet of plywood through the hall and into the ballroom.

He'd been away for months; there wasn't a thing that wouldn't wait another twenty minutes.

He fetched his overnight bag from the car, then headed for the stairs.

His foot was on the first step when the sound of a woman's voice drifting from the drawing room riveted him to the spot.

'I like to start with the colours, Lucy.'

He dropped the bag, moved closer. Heard someone else say, 'This is going to be a spring wedding, so…what? Primroses, daffodils… Yellow?'

'No.' The word was snapped out. Then, more gently, 'Not yellow. April is getting late for daffodils. I did see violets as I drove in through the wood, though. Why don't you take a tour of the exhibitors and bring me anything and everything you can find from deepest violet through to palest mauve? With just a touch of green, I think.'

'Anything special?'

'Ribbons, jewellery, accessories. Ask the florist what he'll have available. And don't forget to make a note of where everything came from…'

She had her back to him, standing shadowed by the deep embrasure of the door as she quietly absorbed everything that was going on but, long before she turned, stepped forward into the sunlight streaming in through front doors propped wide open for workmen carrying in a load of steel trestles, he knew exactly who that voice belonged to.

He'd spent an entire afternoon listening to it as they'd gone, item by item, through her account. Watching her unbutton her jacket. Moisten her lips.

All the time he'd been away it hadn't been Candy's last-minute change of heart that had kept him from sleeping.

It had been the flush on Sylvie Smith's cheeks. The memory of long legs, a glimpse of lace.

Her hot body moulded to his.

Her pitiful tears.

Her tears had haunted him, plaguing him with guilt, but now he understand that her tears had not been for what he'd done to her, but because she'd just risked everything she had in a momentary rush of lust. No wonder she couldn't wait to get away…

Sylvie smiled encouragingly at the youthful journalist, the advance guard from *Celebrity* whose job it was to research background and photo opportunities so that when the photographer arrived on Sunday there would be no waiting. And to encourage her to give her imagination free rein when it came to the fantasy wedding.

Full of enthusiasm, the girl immediately set about hunting down anything she could find in the chosen colour scheme.

Sylvie, not in the least bit enthusiastic, dropped the face-aching smile that seemed to have been fixed ever since she'd arrived at Longbourne Court and looked around at the chaos in what had once been her mother's drawing room.

The furniture had been moved out, stored somewhere to leave room for the exhibitors. But it wasn't the emptiness that tore at her. It was the unexpected discovery that, despite the passing of ten years, so little had changed. It was not the difference but the familiarity that caught at the back of her throat. Tugged at her heart.

The pictures that had once been part of her life were still hanging where they had always been. Velvet curtains, still blue in the deep folds but ever since she could remember faded to a silvery-grey where the light touched them, framed an unchanged view.

There was even a basket of logs in the hearth that might have been there on the day the creditors had seized the house and its contents nearly ten years ago, taking everything to cover the mess that her grandfather, in his attempt to recoup the family fortunes, had made of things.

But driving in the back way through the woods at the crack of dawn, walking in through the kitchen and seeing Mrs Kennedy standing at the sink, her little cry of surprised pleasure, the hug she'd given her while they'd both shed a tear, had been like stepping back in time.

She could almost imagine that her mother had just gone out for an hour or two, would at any moment walk through the door, dogs at her heels…

She swallowed, blinked, reminded herself what was at stake. Forced herself to focus on the job in hand.

She'd already decided that the only way to handle this was to treat herself as if she were one of her own clients. Just one more busy career woman without the time to research the endless details that would make her wedding an event to remember for the rest of her life.

Distancing herself from any emotional involvement.

It was, after all, her job. Something she did every day. Nothing to get excited about. Except, of course, that was just what it should be. Something to be over-the-moon excited about rather than just a going-through-the-motions chore.

She shook her head. The quicker she got on with it, the quicker it would be over. She had the colour scheme, which was a start.

'I'll be in the morning room,' she called out to Lucy, already busily talking to exhibitors, searching out anything useful. It was time she was at work too, hunting down a theme to hang the whole thing on, something original that she hadn't used before.

And the even bigger problem of the dress.

She turned to find her way blocked by six and half feet of broad-shouldered male and experienced a bewildering sense of *déjà vu*.

A feeling that this had happened before.

And then she looked up and realised that it was not an illusion. This *had* happened before, except on that occasion the male concerned had been wearing navy pin-stripe instead of grey cashmere.

'*Some billionaire…*' Laura had said, but hadn't mentioned a name. And she hadn't bothered to ask, pretending she didn't care.

She cared now because it wasn't just 'some' billionaire who'd bought her family home and was planning to turn it into a conference centre.

It was Tom McFarlane, the man with whom, just for a few moments, she'd totally lost it. Whose baby she was carrying. Who'd grabbed her offer to forget it had ever happened. She'd expected at least an acknowledgement…

'Tell me, Miss Smith,' he said while she was still struggling to get her mouth around a simple, Good morning, using exactly the same sardonic tone with which he'd queried every item on her invoice all those months ago. The same look with which he'd reduced her to a stuttering jangle of unrestrained hormones.

Despite everything, she hadn't been able to get that voice, the heat of those eyes, his touch, the weight, heat of his body, out of her head for weeks afterwards.

Make that months.

Maybe not at all…

The man she most wanted to see in the entire world. The man she most dreaded seeing because she'd made a promise and she would have to keep it.

'What?' she demanded, since they were clearly bypassing the civilities, but then there had never been anything civil between them. Only something raw, almost primitive. 'What do you want?'

Stupid question…

He didn't want anything from her.

'To know what you're doing here.' Then, presumably just to ram the point home, because he must surely know that it had once been her home, 'In my house.'

'It's yours?' she said, managing to feign surprise. 'I was told some billionaire had bought it but no one thought to mention your name. But then I didn't ask.' And because she had nothing to apologise for—she'd not only been invited here, but was taking part in this nonsense at great personal inconvenience and no little expense—she said, 'If you'll excuse me, Mr McFarlane?'

She'd been so right to keep it businesslike.

He didn't move, but continued to regard her with those relentlessly fierce eyes that were apparently hell-bent on scrambling her brains.

The man she'd dreaded seeing. The man she'd longed more than anything to see, talk to. If he would just give her a chance, let her show him a scan of the baby they'd made. His daughter. But maybe he understood the risk, the danger of being sucked into a relationship he'd never asked for, never wanted.

She'd given him that get-out-of-jail-free card and could not take it back. And, since he was studiously avoiding the subject, clearly he had no intention of voluntarily surrendering it.

'I have a lot to get through today,' she said, unable to bear it another moment and indicating that she wanted to pass. She'd meant to sound brisk and decisive but the effect was undermined by a slight wobble on the 'h-h-have'.

She might have a lot to get through but the dress would have to wait until she'd had enough camomile tea to drown the squadron of butterflies that were practising formation flying just below her midriff.

Except that it wasn't butterflies but her baby girl practising dance steps.

His baby girl…

'I don't think so,' he responded, not moving.

Well, no. She hadn't for a moment imagined it would be that easy. Trapped in the doorway, she had no choice but to wait.

'What are you doing here?' he repeated.

A man came through the front door carrying a pile of chairs and Tom McFarlane moved to let him pass, taking a step closer so that she was near enough for the warmth of his body to reach out and touch her.

The warmth had taken her by surprise the first time; she would have sworn that he was stone-cold right through until he'd put his hands around her waist, slid his palms against the bare skin of her back and his mouth had come down on hers, heating her to the bone.

Not cold. Anything but cold. More like a volcano—the kind with tiny wisps of smoke escaping through fumaroles, warning that the smallest disturbance could bring it to turbulent, boiling life.

Her only escape was to retreat, take a step back. His eyes, gleaming dangerously, suggested it would be the safe move, but she knew better.

She wasn't the naïve girl who'd left this house nearly ten years ago. She'd made a life for herself; had used what skills she had to build a successful business. She hadn't done that by backing away from difficult situations, but by confronting them.

She knew he'd take retreat as a sign of weakness so, difficult as it was, she stood her ground.

Even when he continued to challenge her with a look that sent the butterflies swerving, diving, performing aerial loop the loops.

'In the middle of a Wedding Fayre?' he persisted, when she didn't answer.

He didn't sound particularly happy about that. He'd be even less so if he knew why she was part of it. They were in agreement about that, anyway. Not that it helped.

'I'm, um, working. It's a *Celebrity* thing,' she said, offering the barest minimum in the hope that he wouldn't be interested in the details. 'They're covering this event.'

'I'd heard,' he said, leaning back slightly, propping an elbow in one hand while rubbing a darkly stubbled chin in urgent need of a shave with the other as he regarded her with a thoughtful frown. 'So what kind of feature would a wedding planner be working on for a gossip magazine?'

Of course he was interested.

Men like Tom McFarlane—women like her—did not succeed by glossing over the details.

'I don't just coordinate weddings,' she replied. 'SDS, my company, organises all kinds of events. Celebrations. Bonding weekends for company staff. Conferences…'

At this point she would normally offer to send a brochure.

She fought the temptation, but only because she'd have to explain to Laura how she came to be thrown out of what had once been her family home.

'And which of those events is being featured by *Celebrity?*'

He spread his fingers in a gesture so minimal that it made the word redundant but which, nevertheless, perfectly expressed his meaning. 'At a Wedding Fayre.'

She shifted her shoulders, sketching an equally minimal shrug while she tried to come up with an answer that wouldn't send him through the roof.

Rescue came in the form of Pam Baxter, approaching from the kitchen.

'Tom?' she said, evidently surprised to see him. 'You're still here. I've just asked Mrs Kennedy to make you some breakfast.' Then, looking to see who he was talking to, 'Oh, hi, Sylvie,' she said, spotting her in the shadows of the doorway. 'Have you introduced yourself to—'

'There was no need—' Tom McFarlane cut short her introduction '—Miss Smith and I have already met. In her professional capacity.'

'Oh?' Then, belatedly catching on to his meaning, 'Oh.' She might have added something else under her breath. Neither of them asked her to speak up. In fact no one said anything for what seemed like a very long time until Pam broke the silence with, 'Have you settled in, Sylvie? Got everything you need?'

'Settled in?' Tom McFarlane demanded before she could reply, never taking his eyes off her.

'Sylvie's wedding is being featured by *Celebrity* magazine,' Pam said, which saved her the bother of having to give him the bad news.

'Her wedding?'

The silver specks in the rock-grey eyes turned molten. He was angry. Well, of course he was angry. He probably thought she'd arranged the whole thing, had brought it to his doorstep in an attempt to force his hand.

'They're giving Sylvie's charity a vast amount of money for the chance to feature it,' Pam said before she could do anything, say anything to reassure him. 'She was going to stay in Melchester, but it seemed so much more sensible to have her stay here. It's not as if we're short of rooms.'

'Her charity?' He turned away to look at Pam and for a moment Sylvie was assailed by a curious mixture of emotions. Relief, largely. But something else. Something almost like *loss*...

As if being looked at by Tom McFarlane brought her to life. Which would explain why, ever since she'd had to leave him, taking delivery of that damn cake, she'd felt something had been missing.

'The Pink Ribbon Club? Sylvie's mother, Lady Annika Duchamp Smith, founded it.'

'Your father was *that* Mr Smith?' he said.

For a moment Tom McFarlane had been distracted, but now he regarded her with, if that was possible, even more dislike.

Something missing? That would be her common sense, obviously.

'Yes,' she said shortly. 'He was that Mr Smith.'

'And now the charity is yours.'

'I took my mother's place as the Honorary President, that's all. I help with fund-raising when I can. Like now.'

'So you used to live here?'

She'd misjudged him over that. He hadn't known. But he did now.

'Well, yes,' she said, doing her best to imply a good-heaven's-that-was-years-ago carelessness. As if it didn't matter. Adding, with polite interest, 'I understand that the plan is to turn the place into a conference centre.'

'And where did you hear that?'

'From someone who lives locally who's involved with English Heritage.' She gave a little shrug. 'You can't keep secrets in the country, Mr McFarlane.'

'No?'

There was something almost threatening in the word. A warning.

Ignoring it, striving for casual, as if it *really* didn't matter to her what he did with the house, she said, 'Are you telling me it isn't true?'

'Oh, it's true,' he assured her, with what could only be described as a satisfied little smile—nowhere near big enough to get anywhere near his eyes—which suggested that she needed to work on her 'carelessness'. 'Do you have a problem with that?'

'Not at all—'

'A rare moment of agreement—'

'—in fact I was going to offer my company's conference services. I'll ask my office to send you a brochure, shall I?'

That, at least, got a reaction. A glowering, furious reaction but Pam stepped in before it boiled over with a swift interjection.

'I'd better go and put your breakfast on hold for another twenty minutes. Sylvie? Can I get you something?'

'Thanks, but I don't need waiting on, Pam,' she said. 'I know my way about.' Which was probably exactly the wrong thing to say but she doubted that there was anything she could say that was right.

Realising that this was a conversation going downhill fast, Pam took charge. 'It's no trouble. Camomile tea, isn't it?' And, before she could say anything else calculated to irritate her boss, 'You're okay in the morning room? It's warm enough?'

'It's perfect. Thank you.'

Pam waited, evidently planning to escort her out of harm's way, but, still trapped in the doorway by Tom McFarlane's rock-like figure, she was unable to escape so, with a meaningful look at him, she said, 'Shout if you need anything, Sylvie.' And left them to it.

'So, Miss Duchamp Smith—'

'Just Smith. Sylvie,' she added with a touch of desperation—

how ridiculous was that? It didn't elicit an invitation to call him Tom and, since she was the one in the wrong place, she said, 'I promise you that I had no idea that it was your company that had bought Longbourne Court, Mr McFarlane.' She emphasized the Mr McFarlane, making the point that she wasn't here to put in a plea for her baby. Or for herself. 'If I'd known—'

He didn't wait for her to tell him that she wouldn't have accepted Pam's invitation to stay. He simply leaned close and, speaking very softly, said, 'Well, you do now, so you won't get too comfortable in the morning room, will you? Or upstairs. I've had my fill of your kind.'

She didn't have to ask what kind of woman he thought she was. Twenty per cent told her that and how could she protest when the last time they'd been this close he'd had one hand on her naked back and the other had just found the gap between stocking and the lace of her Agent Provocateur French knickers and nothing about her response had suggested she was anything but happy about it…

'I promise you,' she snapped back, her cheeks flaming, 'getting comfortable is the last thing on my mind.' Then, lifting her hand in a gesture that indicated she'd like to move and that she wanted enough space to do it without the risk of physical contact, she said, 'If you'll excuse me, the sooner I get started, the sooner I'll be out of here.'

And, finally, she'd managed to say something right because, without another word, he stepped back, allowing her to escape.

CHAPTER FIVE

TOM watched as, head held high, Sylvie Smith walked quickly away.

At their last meeting she'd arrived buttoned up for business in a designer suit, hair coiled up in some elegant style, make-up immaculate, but it hadn't taken her long to start unbuttoning, loosening up. For those big silvery-blue eyes, smoked with heat, to be sending out an unmistakable message, apparently as incapable as him of resisting the attraction between them.

Today he'd caught her unawares, casually dressed in soft dusky-pink layers that all but disguised her condition, her hair caught back with a matching chiffon scarf. Not a button in sight.

She'd been less obviously flirtatious and yet the look had still been there, he thought, his gaze drifting down over hips that were curvier than he remembered, wide-legged trousers that flapped a little as she strode briskly in the direction of the morning room, drawing attention to her comfortable flat shoes.

But he didn't need the short skirt and high heels to feel the same tug of heat that had caught him on the raw a year ago, when he'd walked into her office behind Candy.

When his marriage plans had fallen apart he'd responded by giving her a bad time. Not that she hadn't deserved it.

Then, stupidly, he'd just responded.

He'd done his best to kill the flame, but six months on, his body, driven, denied for months, was on fire again.

The only difference was that this time she was the one getting married.

Concentrate…

Forget Tom McFarlane. Forget that she'd jumped every time the phone rang for weeks after she'd had to race away to save her client from wrecking her own party.

After she'd gone back to find his flat empty. That, after the passion, he'd still gone on his honeymoon for one…

Cold. He was cold…

Beneath the fire there was only ice, she reminded herself.

The raw sexual attraction that had been so unexpected, so new to her, had, for him, been no more than an instinctive male response to a situation charged with tension. An atavistic need to prove his masculinity in the face of rejection.

It hadn't been *personal*.

If she hadn't believed it then, had clung to that hope despite reality, he'd certainly gone out of his way to make sure she understood his feelings this morning.

I've had my fill of your kind…

Her kind being women like Candy Harcourt. Two of a kind. Not.

The truth of the matter was that he didn't know a thing about her. Didn't want to know. Wasn't interested.

Sylvie dragged her gaze away from the familiar distant view of the old village, nestled in the valley bottom alongside the river. The square Norman tower of the church. Forced herself, instead, to look at the photographs provided by the designer who was going to pull out all the stops to provide her with her dream dress.

There was just one problem.

No dream.

Not one with a possibility of coming true, anyway.

She was going to have to be content with the one she had. The one she'd already fulfilled when she'd taken control of her own destiny, refusing ever again to allow her fate to be dictated by circumstances over which she had no control. Or thought she had. She laid a hand against her belly as her baby moved as if to remind her that fate had a way of mocking those who thought they'd beaten her, turning the pages of the album with the other, hoping for something, anything.

A gut response that said 'this one'.

It shouldn't matter, but stupidly it did. If she was going to lay out her fantasy for the world to judge, it had to be real. Perfect.

There's no such thing as perfect…

The 'gut response' wasn't working. It was fully occupied coping with her unexpected confrontation with Tom McFarlane. He looked thinner. Tanned, but thinner. Harder, if that was possible. His features chiselled back to the bone…

She shut her eyes in an attempt to block out the image. Concentrate on the dress. Style… She should stick with style because the wedding dress, as she always reminded her brides, should be an extension of your natural look.

Your wedding day was not a moment to experiment with a fashion statement.

Especially if the result was going to be splashed, in full colour, across the pages of *Celebrity.*

Geena Wagner, the designer showing at the Fayre, was incredibly talented and her gowns were all, without exception, beautiful.

Something like the flowing, beaded and embroidered silk chiffon kaftan-style dress might well have been her choice if she'd been thinking of a beach wedding.

She paused to make a note on her PDA for Josie. She had a bride who was considering that option.

Unfortunately, while the idea of a runaway wedding for two on some deserted beach might be deeply appealing, her task— and she'd had little choice but to accept it—was to include as many exhibitors as possible, which meant it would have to be a traditional wedding.

The whole village church, bells and choir job, with brides- maids, ushers, fancy transport, a marquee fit for a maharajah and more flowers than Kew Gardens.

It should have been a piece of cake. She'd done it before. Sit- ting in this room, making lists, her mother offering suggestions. She wasn't that girl any more…

At least she'd made a start with the flowers, she thought, reaching out for the tiny posy of violets that Lucy—taking her task very seri- ously—had gone out into the park to pick for her. Sweet-scented purple velvet flowers, heart-shaped leaves, tied with narrow purple ribbon. She lifted it to breathe in the scent and for a moment smiled.

Her bridal flowers would be a simple posy of violets. Maybe she could set a new trend for simplicity, she thought, returning to the photographs. A minimalist wedding. Very classy.

The strapless cleavage-enhancing dresses were almost too minimalist, but while perfect for a civil ceremony in some glam- orous setting, wouldn't work in the village church. Or maybe it just wouldn't work for her.

And yet the look would have to be show-stopping.

She needed a theme, something that would tie everything to- gether, or the feature risked being no more than a series of pho- tographs of things…

She sighed, poked amongst the collection of goodies Lucy had found for her. Held a long amethyst earring against her neck. A scrap of smoky mauve chiffon. Ribbons, dried flower petals, in- vitation cards with envelopes lined with lilac tissue.

All utterly gorgeous, but she'd done all that love's young

dream, happy ever after, fairy tale thing ten years ago. Had seen it crumble to dust the minute there was trouble.

Maybe that was why she'd been hit so hard by the Candida Harcourt/Tom McFarlane debacle. It had been too close to home. Had brought back too many painful memories. Despite Tom McFarlane's move on her, it was obvious that he hadn't been over it, he'd just been hurting.

Her response had been to shift the hands-on wedding stuff to Josie, using her pregnancy as an excuse. Not that the clients were getting second-best. Josie was brilliant at making things run on oiled wheels behind the scenes. In fact, if she wasn't very careful, her rivals would be headhunting her, offering her all kinds of incentives to come and work for them.

She made a note on her PDA to do something about that. Which was just another way of putting off the task in hand.

'Come on, Sylvie,' she muttered, taking a couple of long, slow, calming breaths. 'You can do this.'

And then, avoiding the dresses, she picked up one of a pair of embroidered and beaded purple silk shoes.

'Anything catch your eye?' Geena said from the doorway.

'These shoes?' she offered.

'You're finding it difficult?'

She indicated her shape. 'Just a bit. But I've definitely ruled out the vestal virgin look,' she said, indicating the photograph in front of her. 'Not that it isn't lovely,' she added quickly. 'They're all lovely but, to be honest, I'm finding it hard and it's not the bump. It's just not real, you know?' She tried to think of some way to explain. 'I find most of my brides are thinking about their groom when they choose their dress.' Most of them. 'When they find the dress of their dreams they always say something like, "He'll just melt when he sees me in this…"'

Candy, on the other hand, had said, 'Everyone I know will die of envy when they see me in this…' But then that had been the standard by which she'd judged everything about her wedding. Not what Tom would think but how envious everyone else would be.

Maybe that was the difference between marrying for money and marrying for love. Candy hadn't needed any of the trappings when she'd married Quentin. Just the two of them had been enough.

She'd read all about it in their 'true love' story in *Celebrity*.

'You know it's going to be perfect when they say that, don't you?' Geena agreed, breaking into her thoughts. But then, dressing brides was her business so clearly she understood better than most.

'It does help,' Sylvie said. Then shrugged. 'I don't know. Maybe I've planned too many "perfect" weddings that didn't last.'

'Think about the ones that have,' she said, taking the shoe, looking at it. 'This is totally gorgeous.' She tried it on but it was too small and she handed it to Sylvie. 'Go on, your feet are smaller than mine. Try it.'

Anything was better than looking at wedding dresses and the shoe *was* fabulous. She slipped it on and extended her foot. The colour glowed. A few small beads set amongst the rich embroidery caught the light and sparkled.

They both sighed.

'I think we have a bit of a Cinderella moment here,' Geena said with a grin. 'Try the other one. Walk about…' Then, after a moment, 'Are you getting anything?'

'A total reluctance to take them off, give them back,' she admitted, laughing, 'but honestly, purple shoes!'

'Colour is making a big impact in wedding gowns these days,' she said thoughtfully. 'It might work. Embroidery? Appliqué? I have a woman who is brilliant at that.' Then, getting no encouragement, 'What we really need to get you in the mood is a man.'

'I'm sorry, I can't help you there,' she said, concentrating on the shoes.

'No? Really? But what about—'

'Believe it,' Sylvie swiftly cut in. 'The infant is the result of a…a…sperm donation.'

'At a clinic?' She did not sound convinced.

'Not quite, but the man wasn't included in the deal.'

'Oh, well, not to worry. He doesn't have to be "the one",' she said, making little quotation marks. 'Just someone hot enough to get you in that dreamy, this-will-make-him-melt mood.' Then, when she shook her head, 'A this-will-make-him-want-to-tear-it-off-and-take-you-to-bed mood would do,' she assured her.

Which fired up all those visions of Tom McFarlane that she'd been doing her best to smother.

'Not possible, I'm afraid.'

'No? Shame. But there are some seriously hunky blokes putting up a marquee out there. I'll go and drag one of them in, shall I?'

She turned as someone cleared his throat behind her.

'Oh, hi, Mark. What are you doing here?' Then, before he could answer, she glanced at Sylvie, a wicked little gleam in her eye. 'Sylvie, have you met Mark Hilliard, very hot architect of this parish? Mark, Sylvie Smith.'

'You've been misinformed, Sylvie. I live in Upper Haughton with my wife and our three children, so whatever Geena has in mind I regret that the answer is no.'

'My sentiments exactly,' Sylvie said quickly.

But he wasn't finished. 'For this parish you need Tom McFarlane, Geena. The new owner of Longbourne Court.'

And, as the man himself appeared in the doorway, he left them to it while he took his notebook on a tour of the morning room.

'Tom?' Geena said, offering her hand. 'Geena Wagner.' Then, she stood back to admire the view. 'Oh, *yes*. You're perfect.'

'I am?' he asked, confused but smiling. A natural smile, the kind any man would bestow on an attractive woman at their first meeting. The kind he'd never given her.

He hadn't caught sight of her—yet.

Sylvie struggled to protest, but only managed a groan—enough to attract his attention. The confusion remained, but the smile disappeared as fast as a snowball tossed into hell.

'Absolutely perfect!' Geena exclaimed in reply to his question, although he didn't appear to have heard. 'You're not married, are you?' Geena pressed, apparently oblivious to the sudden tension, unaware of the looming disaster.

'Why don't you ask Miss Smith?' he replied while she was still trying to untangle her vocal cords. Stop Geena from making things a hundred times worse.

The mildness of his tone belied the hard glitter in his eyes as he looked over Geena's head and straight at her. As if the fact that he wasn't was somehow *her* fault.

Along with global warming, the national debt and the price of fuel, no doubt.

'You know each other! *Excellent.* The thing is, Tom, Sylvie needs a stand-in fantasy man. Are you game?'

'Nnnnnn…' was all she could manage, since not only were her vocal cords in a knot, but her tongue had apparently turned into a lump of wood.

'That rather depends on the nature of the fantasy,' he replied, ignoring her frantically shaking head. His expression suggested that he harboured any number of fantasies in which she was the main participant…

'Well, all I need is for you to stand there looking hot and fanciable.' She smiled encouragingly. Then, before he could move, 'That's it. Perfect.'

'I didn't do anything,' he protested.

'You don't have to,' she said, grinning hugely at her own cleverness. 'Right, Sylvie. Get your imagination into gear.'

'Geena, I think…'

'Thinking is the last thing I want from you. This is all about feelings. The senses,' she said bossily, stepping from between them and, taking her by the shoulders, lined her up so that she was facing him.

The sun was streaming into the morning room and she'd shrugged off the loose knee-length cardigan-style wrap that had become a permanent cover-up since her pregnancy had begun to show and her condition was unmistakable.

And his expression left her in no doubt as to his feelings. He was angry…

'Forget that sweater, those pants, excellent though they are,' Geena said. 'For this exercise he's wearing a morning suit…' she glanced down at the purple shoes '…a grey morning suit with a purple waistcoat and violets in his buttonhole.'

Tom McFarlane made a sound that suggested 'not in this life'.

'He's standing at the altar and he's—'

'What altar?' Tom demanded, having been finally jerked out of his own private fantasy world in which, no doubt, all wedding coordinators were fed on wedding cake—the kind with rock-hard royal icing—until their teeth fell out.

What had he done with that wedding cake…?

'Good point, Tom. Village church, Sylvie?' she asked, breathing into her thoughts.

Sylvie opened her mouth, determined to put an end to this nightmare, but it was apparently a rhetorical question because Geena swept on without waiting for an answer.

'Where else? But you don't have to worry about that, Tom.'

'I don't?' he said, apparently unconvinced, but Geena was in full flow and nothing, it seemed, was going to stop her.

'Absolutely not. We're doing all the work here.'

Sylvie shrugged helplessly as Tom McFarlane lifted a brow in her direction, putting them, for the briefest moment, on the same side.

Not possible.

In the middle of the night she might have succumbed to the impossible dream. The happy ever after. But that was all it had ever been—a dream.

'Okay, Sylvie. The church doorway is decorated with ever-greens and flowers. Your bridesmaids are waiting. All adults?' she asked. 'Or will you be having children too?'

Concentrate on the wedding. Just make the most of this fantasy moment...

'One adult,' she said. If this were real, she'd want Josie in the rear, running things. Parting her from her boots might be diffi-cult, but at least her hair already matched the colour scheme. 'Assorted children. Four girls, one boy.'

Her fantasy should, after all, be as close to reality as possible and she had four god-daughters who would never forgive her if they were excluded from the big day. And a five-year-old godson who would probably never forgive her if he was expected to appear in public in a pair of satin breeches. But he'd look sweet and his sisters could use the threat of posting the photographs on the Internet to keep him in order when he was at that difficult age—the one between five and ninety-five.

Girls needed all the edge they could get, she thought, as she stopped fighting a deep need for this and just let herself go.

'Okay, here's the scene,' Geena said. 'The organ strikes up, your father takes your arm...'

'No!' Last time that had been her grandfather's role. This time there was no one. 'I'll be on my own,' she said, doing what Geena had said. Not thinking. Just feeling.

Realising that both Geena and Tom were looking at her a little oddly, she said, 'I'm an adult. I don't need anyone to give me away.'

'Oh, right… Well, whatever. It's your wedding. So you're poised to walk up the aisle.' Geena picked up the violets, pressed them into her hand. 'Okay, the organ strikes up, you hear the rustle as everyone in the church gets to their feet. This is it. Da da da-da…' she sang. 'You're walking up the aisle. Walk, walk,' she urged, pushing her towards Tom. 'Everyone is looking at you. People are sighing, but you don't see them, don't hear them,' she went on relentlessly. 'Everything is concentrated on the only two people in the church who matter. You, in the dress of your dreams,' she said. 'And him.'

She met Tom McFarlane's gaze.

Why was he still there? Why hadn't he just turned around and walked out? He didn't have to stay…

'What does it feel like as you move, Sylvie?' Geena murmured, very softly, as if they were truly in church. 'Cool against your skin? Can you feel the drag of a train? Can you hear it rustle? Tell me, Sylvie. Tell me what you're feeling. Tell me what he's seeing…'

For a moment she was there in the cool church with the sun streaming in through the stained glass. Could feel the dress as it brushed against her legs. The antique lace of her grandmother's veil…

Could see Tom McFarlane standing in the spangle of coloured light, looking at her as if she made his world whole as she walked down the aisle towards him, a simple posy of violets in her hand.

'Tell me what he's seeing that's making him melt,' Geena persisted.

His gaze dropped to the unmistakable bulge where his baby was growing beneath her heart and, shattering the illusion, said,

'Sackcloth and ashes would do it.' Then, turning abruptly away, 'Mark, have you got everything you need in here?'

He didn't wait for an answer but, leaving the architect to catch up, he walked out, as if being in the same room with her was more than he could bear.

Mark, his smile wry, said, 'Nice one, Geena. If you need any help getting your foot out of your mouth I can put you in touch with a good osteopath.' Then, 'Good meeting you, Sylvie.'

Geena, baffled, just raised a hand in acknowledgement as he left, then said, 'What on earth was his *problem?*'

Sylvie, reaching for the table as her knees buckled slightly, swallowed, then, forcing herself to respond casually, said, 'It would have been a good idea to have asked where we met.'

When she didn't rush to provide the information, Geena gestured encouragingly. 'Well? Where did you meet?'

'I went to school with the woman he was going to marry, so I was entrusted with the role of putting together her fantasy wedding. I did try to warn you.'

'But I was too busy talking. It's a failing,' she admitted. 'So what was with the sackcloth and ashes remark? What did you do—book the wrong church? Did the marquee collapse? The guests go down with food poisoning? What?'

'The bride changed her mind three days before the wedding.'

'You're kidding!' Then, glancing after him, 'Was she crazy?'

'Rather the opposite. She came to her senses just in time. Candy Harcourt?' she prompted. Then, when Geena shook her head, 'You don't read the gossip magazines?'

'Is it compulsory?'

Sylvie searched for a laugh but failed to find one. He knew and she'd seen his reaction.

While there had been only silence, she had been able to fool herself that he might, given time, come round. Not any more.

It couldn't get any worse.

'No, it's not compulsory, Geena, but in this instance I rather wish you had.'

'I still don't understand his problem,' she said, frowning. 'You can't be held responsible for the bride getting cold feet.'

'She eloped with one of my staff.'

'Ouch.' She shrugged. Then, as the man himself walked across the lawn in front of the window, 'I still think that taking it out on you is a little harsh and if I didn't have my own fantasy man waiting at home I'd be more than happy to give him a talking to he wouldn't forget in a hurry. Although, to be honest, from the way he looked at you—'

'I believe the expression "if looks could kill" just about covers it,' Sylvie cut in quickly, distracting Geena before she managed to connect the dots.

'Only if spontaneous combustion was the chosen method of execution. Are you sure it was only the bride who fell for the wedding planner?' she pressed. Then perhaps realising just what she was saying, she held up her hands, in a gesture of apology. 'Will you do me a favour and forget I said that? Forget I even thought it. How bad would it be for business if brides got the impression they couldn't trust you with their grooms?'

'What? No!' she declared, but felt the betraying heat rush to her cheeks.

Geena didn't pursue it, however—although she had an eyebrow that spoke volumes—just said, 'My mistake.' But not with any conviction—she was clearly a smart woman. Her sense of self-preservation belatedly kicked in, however, and she said, 'Okay, forget Mr Hot-and-Sexy for the moment and just tell me what you saw.'

'Saw?'

'Just now. I was watching you. You saw something. Felt something.'

What she'd seen was the image that Geena had put into her head. Her nineteen-year-old self dressed in her great-grandmother's wedding dress, the soft lace veil falling nearly to her feet.

The only difference being that in her fantasy moment it hadn't been the man she'd been going to marry standing at the altar.

It had been Tom McFarlane who, for just a moment, she'd been certain was about to reach out and take her hand...

'Sylvie?'

'Yes,' she said quickly. 'You're right. I was remembering something. A dress...'

Concentrate on the dress.

'Are you really going to be able to make something from scratch in a few days?' she asked a touch desperately. 'Normally it takes weeks. Months...'

'Well, I admit that it's going to be a bit of a midnight oil job, but this is the world's biggest break for me and everyone in the workroom is on standby to pull out all the stops to give you what you want.' Then, 'Besides, since you're not actually going to be walking up the aisle in it—at least not this week—it wouldn't actually matter if there was a strategic tack or pin in place for the photographs, would it?'

'That rather depends where you put the pins!'

'Forget the pins. Come on,' she urged. 'This is fantasy time! Indulge yourself, Sylvie. Dream a little. Dream a lot. Give me something I can work with...'

Those kind of dreams would only bring her heartache, but this was important for Geena and she made a determined effort to play along.

'Actually, the truth is not especially indulgent,' she said with a rueful smile. 'Or terribly helpful. I did the fantasy for real when I was nineteen. On that occasion the plan was to wear my great-grandmother's wedding dress.'

'Really? Gosh, that's so romantic.'

Yes, well, nineteen was an age for romance. She knew better now…

'So, let's see. We're talking nineteen-twenties? Ankle-bone length? Dropped waist? Lace?' She took out a pad and did a quick sketch. 'Something like that?'

'Pretty much,' she said, impressed. 'That's lovely.'

'Thank you.' Then, shaking her head. 'You are so lucky. How many people even know what their great-grandmother was wearing when she married, let alone still have the dress? You *have* still got it?'

About to shake her head, explain, Sylvie realised that it was probably just where she'd left it. After all, nothing else seemed to have been touched.

But that was a step back to a different life. A different woman.

'I'm supposed to be displaying your skills, Geena,' she said. 'Giving you a showcase for your talent. A vintage gown wouldn't do that.'

'You're supposed to be giving the world your personal fantasy,' Geena reminded her generously. 'Although, unless it's been stored properly, it's likely to be moth-eaten and yellowed. Not quite what *Celebrity* are expecting for their feature. And, forgive me for mentioning this, but I don't imagine your great-grandmother was—how do they put it?—in an "interesting condition" when she took that slow walk up the aisle.'

'True.' The dress had been stored with care and when she'd been nineteen it had been as close to perfect as it was possible for a dress to be. Life had moved on. She was a different woman now and, pulling a face, she said, 'Rising thirty and pregnant, all that virginal lace would look singularly inappropriate.'

'Actually, I've got something rather more grown-up in mind for you,' she replied. 'Something that will go with those shoes.

But I'd really love to see your grandmother's dress, if only out of professional interest.'

'I'll see what I can do.'

'Great. Now, hold still and I'll run this tape over you and take some measurements so that we can start work on the toile.'

CHAPTER SIX

MARK HILLIARD didn't say a word when Tom joined him, but then they'd known one another for a long time. A look was enough.

'I'm sorry about that. As you may have realised, there's a bit of…tension.'

'Sackcloth and ashes? If that's tension, I wouldn't like to be around when you declare open war.' Mark's smile was thoughtful. 'To be honest, it sounded more like—'

'Like what?' he demanded, but the man just held up his hands and shook his head. But then, he didn't have to say what he was thinking. It was written all over his face. 'It was a business matter,' he said abruptly. Which was true. 'Nothing else.' Which was not.

Sackcloth and ashes.

That wasn't like any business dispute he'd ever been involved in. It was more like an exchange between two people who couldn't make up their minds whether to throttle one another or tear each other's clothes off.

Which pretty much covered it. At least from his viewpoint, except that he hadn't wanted to feel that way about anyone. Out of control. Out of his mind. Racked with guilt…

She had clearly wasted no time in putting him out of her mind. But he could scarcely blame her for that. He'd walked away, hadn't written, hadn't called, then messed up by asking his secretary to send her a cheque for the full amount of her account. Paid in full. No wonder she'd sent the money back.

And then, when he'd been ready to fall at her feet, grovel, it had been too late.

But six months hadn't changed a thing. Sylvie Smith still got to him in ways that he didn't begin to understand.

And he was beginning to suspect, despite the fact that she was expecting a baby with her childhood sweetheart—and he tried not to think about how long that relationship had been in existence, whether it was an affair with her that had wrecked the new Earl's marriage—it was the same for her.

The truth of the matter was that, even in sackcloth, she would have the ability to bring him to meltdown. Which was a bit like getting burned and then putting your hand straight back in the fire.

But as she'd stood there while that crazy female went on about the village church, about walking up the aisle, about someone standing at the altar—about *him* standing at the altar—he'd seen it all as plainly as if he'd been there. Even the light streaming through a stained glass window and dancing around her hair, staining it with a rainbow of colours.

He'd seen it and had wanted to be there in a way he'd never wanted that five-act opera of a wedding, unpaid advertising in the gossip magazines for Miss Sylvie Duchamp Smith that Candy had been planning.

A small country church with the sweet scent of violets that even out here seemed to cling to him instead of some phoney show-piece. A commitment that was *real* between two people who were marrying for all the right reasons.

So real, in fact, that he'd come within a heartbeat of reaching out a hand to her.

Maybe Pam was right. He should go back to London until this was all over. Except he knew it wouldn't help; at least here he would be forced to witness her making plans for her own wedding. The 'blooming' bride. Blooming, glowing…

Euphemisms.

The word was *pregnant*.

If nothing else did it, that fact alone should force him to get a grip on reality.

Realising that Mark was looking at him a little oddly, he turned abruptly and began to walk towards the outbuildings.

'Let's take a look at the coach house and stable block,' he said briskly.

Pregnant.

'I think we could probably get a dozen accommodation units out of the buildings grouped around the courtyard,' Mark said, falling in beside him.

'That sounds promising. What about the barn?'

'There are any number of options open to you there. It's very adaptable. In fact, I did wonder if you'd like to convert it into your own country retreat. There's a small private road and, with a walled garden, it would be very private.'

If it had been anywhere else, he might have been tempted. But Longbourne Court was now a place he just wanted to develop for maximum profit so that he could eradicate it from his memory, along with Sylvie Smith.

The last thing Sylvie had done before she'd left Longbourne Court was to pack the wedding dress away where it belonged, in a chest in the attic containing the rest of her great-grandmother's clothes.

Not wanted in this life.

It was going to be painful to see it again. To touch it. Feel the connection with that part of her which had been packed away with the dress.

Always supposing the chests and trunks were still there.

There was only one way to find out, but Longbourne Court was no longer her home; she couldn't just take the back stairs that led up to the storage space under the roof and start rootling around without as much as a by-your-leave.

But as soon as she'd talked to Josie, reassured herself that everything was running smoothly in her real life, she went in search of Pam Baxter, planning to clear it with her. Get it over with while Tom McFarlane was still safely occupied with the architect.

She'd seen him from the window. Had watched him walking down to the old coach house with Mark Hilliard.

He'd shaved since their last encounter. Changed. The sweater was still cashmere, but it was black.

Like his mood.

And yet he'd had a smile for Geena. The real thing. No wonder the woman had been swept away.

It had been that kind of smile.

The dangerous kind that stirred the blood, heated the skin, brought all kinds of deep buried longings bubbling to the surface.

Not that he'd needed a smile to get that response from her. He'd done it with no more than a look.

But then there had been that look, that momentary connection across Geena's head when, for a fleeting moment, she'd felt as if it were just the two of them against the world. When, for a precious instant, she'd been sure that everything was going to be all right.

No more than wishful thinking, she knew, as she watched a waft of breeze coming up from the river catch at his hair. He dragged his fingers through it, pushing it back off his face before glancing back at the house, at the window of the morning room, as if he felt her watching him.

Frowning briefly before he turned and walked away, leaving Mark to trail in his wake.

She slumped back in the chair, as if unexpectedly released from some crushing grip, and it took all her strength to stand up, to go and find Pam.

The library door was open and when she tapped on it, went in, she discovered the room was empty.

She glanced at her watch, deciding to give it a couple of minutes, crossing without thinking to the shelves, running her hand over the spines of worn, familiar volumes. Everything was exactly as she'd left it. Even the family bible was on its stand and she opened it to the pages that recorded their family history. Each birth, marriage, death.

The blank space beneath her own name for her marriage, her children—that would always remain empty.

The last entry, her mother's death, written in her own hand. After all her mother had been through, that had been so cruel. So unfair. But when had life ever been fair? she thought, looking at the framed photograph standing by itself on a small shelf above the bible.

It was nothing special. Just a group of young men in tennis flannels, lounging on the lawn in front of a tea table on some long ago summer afternoon.

She wasn't sure how long she'd been standing there, hearing the distant echo of her great-grandfather's voice as he'd repeated their names, a roll-call of heroes, when some shift in the air, a prickle at the base of her neck, warned her that she was no longer alone.

Not Pam. Pam would have spoken as soon as she'd seen her.

'Checking up on me, Mr McFarlane?' she asked, not looking round, even when he joined her. 'Making sure I'm not getting too comfortable?'

'Who are these people?' he asked, his voice grating as, ignoring the question, he picked up the photograph and made a gesture with it which—small though it was—managed to include the portraits that lined the stairs, the upper gallery, that hung over fireplaces.

She waited, anticipating some further sarcasm, but when she didn't answer he looked up and for a moment she saw genuine curiosity.

'Just family,' she said simply.

'Family?' He looked as if he would say something more and she held her breath.

'Yes?' she prompted, but his eyes snapped back to the photograph.

'Didn't they have anything better to do than play games?' he demanded. 'Laze about at tea parties?'

Her turn to frown. Something about the photograph disturbed him, she could see, but she couldn't let him get away with that dismissive remark.

Laying a finger on the figure of a young man who was smiling, obviously saying something to whoever was taking the photograph, she said, 'This is my great-uncle Henry. He was twenty-one when this was taken. Just down from Oxford.' She moved to the next figure. 'This is my great-uncle George. He was nineteen. Great-uncle Arthur was fifteen.' She leaned closer so that her shoulder touched his arm, but she ignored the *frisson* of danger, too absorbed in the photograph to heed the warning. 'That's Bertie. And David. They were cousins. The same age as Arthur. And this is Max. He'd just got engaged to my great-aunt Mary. She was the one holding the camera.'

'And the boy in the front? The joker pulling the face?'

'That's my great-grandfather, James Duchamp. He wasn't quite twelve when this was taken. He was just short of his seventeenth birthday four years later when the carnage that they call The Great War ended. The only one of them to survive, marry, raise a family.'

'It was the same for every family,' he said abruptly.

'I know, Mr McFarlane. Rich and poor of all nations died together by the million in the trenches.' She looked up. 'There were precious few tennis parties for anyone after this was taken.'

Tom McFarlane stared at the picture, doing his best to ignore the warmth of her shoulder against his chest, the silky touch of a strand of hair that had escaped her scarf as it brushed against his cheek.

'For most people there never were any tennis parties,' he said as, incapable of moving, physically distancing himself from her, he did his best to put up mental barriers. Then, in the same breath, 'Since we appear to be stuck under the same roof for the next week, it might be easier if you called me Tom. It's not as if we're exactly strangers.' Tearing them down.

'I believe that's exactly what we are, Mr McFarlane,' she replied, cool as the proverbial cucumber. 'Strangers.'

He nodded, acknowledging the truth of that. The lie of it. 'Nevertheless,' he persisted and she glanced up, her look giving the lie to her words as she met his gaze, as if searching for something… 'Just to save time,' he added.

'To save time?'

She didn't quite shrug, didn't quite smile—or only in self-mockery, as if she'd hoped for something more. What, for heaven's sake? Hadn't she got enough?

'Very well,' she said. 'Tom it is. On the strict understanding that it's just to save time. But you are going to have to call me Sylvie. My time may not be as valuable as yours, but it's in equally short supply.'

'I think I can manage that. Sylvie.'

Divorced from 'Duchamp' and 'Smith', the name slipped over his tongue like silk and he wanted to say it again.

Sylvie.

Instead, he cleared his throat and focused on the photograph.

'Why is this here?' he asked. 'Didn't you want it?' Then, because if this had been a photograph of his family, he would never have let it go, 'It's part of your family history.'

Sylvie took the photograph from him. Laid her hand against the cold glass for a moment, her eyes closed, remembering.

'When the creditors moved in,' she said after a moment, 'all I was allowed to take were my clothes and a few personal possessions. The pearls I was given by my grandfather for my eighteenth birthday. And my car, although they insisted on checking the log book to make sure it was in my name before they let me drive away.'

It should have mattered. But by then nothing had mattered…

'You'll understand if I save my sympathy for the people who were owed money.'

She looked up at him. So solid. So successful. So scornful.

'You needn't be concerned for the little men,' she said. 'We always paid our bills. Our problems were caused by two lots of death duties in three years and the fact that my grandfather, after a lifetime of a somewhat relaxed attitude to expenditure, had decided to think of the future, the family and, on the advice of someone he trusted, had become a Lloyds "name" a couple of years before everything went belly-up.'

A fact which, when he realised what it meant, had certainly contributed to the heart attack that had killed him and, indirectly, to the death of her mother.

'The irony of the situation is that if he'd carried on throwing parties and letting the future take care of itself we'd all have been a lot better off,' she added.

'But this photograph doesn't have any value,' he protested. 'Beyond historical interest. Sentimental attachment.'

'Yes, well, they did say that once a complete inventory had been taken I would be allowed to come back, take away family things that had no intrinsic value. But then a world-famous rock star who'd visited the house as a boy was seized by a mission to conserve the place in aspic as a slice of history.'

Tom McFarlane made a sound that suggested he was less than impressed.

'I know. More money than sense, but he made an offer that the creditors couldn't refuse and, since he was prepared to pay a very large premium for his pleasure, he got it all. Family photographs, portraits, all the junk in the attic. Even Mr and Mrs Kennedy, the housekeeper and man of all work, were kept on as caretakers, so it wasn't all bad news.'

'Could they do that? Sell everything?'

'Who was to stop them? I didn't have any money to fight for the rights to my family history and, even if I did, the only people to benefit would have been the lawyers. This way everything was settled. Was preserved.'

And she'd been able to move on, make another life instead of every day being reminded of things she'd rather forget.

Jeremy putting off the wedding—just until things had settled down. Her mother's determination to confront the people who were draining everything out of her family home. Her father... No, she refused to waste a single thought on him.

'I'd moved into a flat share with two other girls by then and had barely enough room to hang my clothes, let alone the family portraits.' She took the photograph from him and replaced it on the shelf where it had been all her life. All her mother's life. All her grandfather's life too. 'Besides, you're right. This isn't just my history. As you said, it was the same for everyone.'

Had he really said that? he wondered as he looked around him.

Longbourne Court was a gracious minor stately home, but from the moment he'd walked through the door Tom had recognised it for what it was. A *family* home. A place where generations of the same family had lived, cradle to grave, each putting their mark on it.

It wasn't just the portraits or the trees in the parkland. It was the scuffs and wear, the dips in the floorboards where countless feet had walked, the patina of polish applied by a hundred different hands. Scratches where dogs had pawed at doors, raced across ancient oak floors.

He realised that Sylvie was frowning, as if his question was beyond her. And it was, of course. How could she know what it was like to have no one? No photographs. No keepsakes.

'Not everyone has memories, a place in history, Sylvie.'

'No memories?' He hadn't mentioned himself and yet she seemed to instantly catch his meaning. 'No family?' Then, 'How dreadful for you, Tom. I'm so sorry.'

She said the words simply, sincerely, his name warm upon her lips. And, for the second time that day, Tom regretted the impulse to speak first and think afterwards. Betraying something within him that he kept hidden, even from himself.

'I don't need your pity,' he said sharply.

'No?' Maybe she recognised the danger of pressing it and, no doubt trained from birth in the art of covering conversational *faux pas,* she quickly moved away and, looking around, said, 'I was hoping to find Pam. I don't suppose you know where she is?'

'Why? What do you want her for? If you're in a hurry, maybe I can help.'

She hesitated, clearly reluctant to say, which no doubt meant it had something to do with this wretched Wedding Fayre. He thought he was hard-nosed when it came to business, but using her own wedding as a promotional opportunity seemed cold even to him.

But, choosing to demonstrate that he was quite as capable as her when it came to covering the awkward moment—at least when he wasn't causing them—he said, 'The truth is I was looking for you in order to apologise for my "sackcloth and ashes" remark. It was inexcusable.'

'On the contrary. You had every excuse,' she said quickly. 'I really should have made more of an effort to stop Geena before she got totally carried away.'

'You might as well have tried to stop a runaway train.'

'True, but even so—'

'Forget it,' he said. 'I should have done it myself, preferably without the crash barrier technique. I'm not normally quite so socially inept, but I'm sure you will understand that you were the last person I expected to see at Longbourne Court.'

And, confronted with the growing evidence of her impending motherhood which, two months on from seeing her on the cover of that hideous magazine, was now obvious, he was trying hard not to think about just how pregnant she was.

Trying not to wonder just how soon after that lost moment with him she'd found the man she wanted to spend the rest of her life with. Someone who was a world away from him. Someone she'd known for ever...

'That makes two of us,' she said. 'You were the very last person I expected to see. Candy told me you disliked the country.'

'I dislike certain aspects of the country. Hunting, shooting,' he added.

'Me too. My great-grandfather banned all field sports from the estate. He said there had been too much killing...' She paused for a heartbeat and then said, 'You did get my letter?'

He nodded and turned away. He should apologise, explain that he hadn't meant it the way she'd taken it. She'd earned every penny of her fee. But what would be the point?

In truth, six months spent thinking about what had happened, about her—whether he'd wanted to or not—had left him with a very clear understanding of his responsibility for what had happened.

He'd known what he was doing when he'd called her to his office.

Had known what he was doing when he'd kept her there, forcing her to go through that wretched account, when, in truth, it had meant nothing to him.

Convinced that she had somehow sabotaged his future, he'd wanted to punish her. The truth was he'd sabotaged his own plans, had become more and more distant from Candy as the wedding had grown nearer, using the excuse of work when the only thing on his mind had been that moment when he'd walked into Sylvie Smith's office and she'd looked up and the smile had died on her lips…

And he'd blamed her for that too.

Then, for just a moment, instead of being a man and woman locked in an ongoing argument, they had been fused, as one, and the world had, briefly, made complete sense—until he'd seen the tears spilling down her cheeks and had known, without the need for words, that he'd got it wrong, that he'd made the biggest mistake of his life.

What good would it do to say any of that now? She had her life mapped out and to tell her how he felt would only make her feel worse. Better that she should despise him than feel sorry for him.

'I'm sorry,' he said. 'For everything.'

She turned away, a faint blush of pink staining her cheeks as, no doubt, like him, she was reliving a moment that had fired not just the body, but something deeper—the mindless heat of two people so lost to sense that nothing could have stopped them.

Or maybe he was just hoping it was that. It was, in all likelihood, plain guilt.

The fact that just six months later she was visibly pregnant with another man's child demonstrated that as nothing else could and he'd done his level best to forget her.

From the first moment he'd set eyes on her he'd done his best to put her out of his mind.

That he'd felt such an immediate, powerful attraction to this woman at their first meeting when Candy, the woman he was about to marry, was standing next to him, had been bad enough and he'd kept his distance, had avoided anything to do with the wedding plans. Had buried himself in work and done his best to avoid thinking about her at all.

He'd made a fair fist of it until she'd waved her presence in front of him with that damned invoice.

If she hadn't added that handwritten 'Personal' to the envelope—no doubt in an attempt to save him embarrassment—his PA would have opened it, dealt with it, would have put through the payment without even troubling him.

Instead, it had been left on his desk to catch him on the raw when he'd opened it. Raw, angry, he had been determined to look her in the eye and challenge her. Challenge himself.

Well, he'd won. And lost.

Twice. Because, face to face with her now, he knew that she was the one. The One.

Then, because that was the last thing he wanted to think about, he said, 'What did you want Pam for?'

She stared at him for a moment, then raised a hand, swiping at the air as if to clear away something he couldn't see, then crossed distractedly to the desk as if she might find her.

'I just wanted to ask her if I could go up into the attics to look for something that belonged to my great-grandmother. To borrow for a little while.'

'Your great-grandmother?' he repeated, grateful for the distraction. 'How long has it been there?'

'Since I put there. Before I left.' She turned back to face him. 'Unless you've already started to clear things?' She made it sound as if he was destroying something beyond price.

Maybe, for her, he was.

'Apart from instructing Mark Hilliard to put in an application for outline planning, I've done nothing,' he assured her, 'and, as far as I can tell from my tour of the place with Mark this morning, nothing appears to have been touched.'

'Oh. Well, that's hopeful.'

She'd begun to soften as they'd talked about her family and for a moment he'd forgotten the barrier between them as, apparently, had she. It was back in place now and it wasn't that edgy barrier with which she'd fought the attraction between them but something colder. Angrier.

'Was this the great-grandmother who married the boy in the photograph?' he asked, using what he'd learned about her. That people, her family, were more important than possessions. Hoping, against all reality, to draw her back to him.

'James. Yes. The other lot, the Smiths, were a soldiering clan so they were constantly on the move and by comparison travelled light.'

She said it dismissively, clearly not a big fan of the Smiths. She hadn't wanted her father at her wedding, at least not walking her down the aisle, he remembered. What was that about?

'From the clutter upstairs, I'd say that's probably a good thing,' he said, making no comment. Then, as if he didn't have another thing in the world to occupy him, 'Do you want to take a look up there now?'

'It is a bit urgent,' she said and glanced, a touch helplessly, at Pam's desk. 'Will Pam be back soon?'

'Not in time to be of any help to you.' For a moment he waited, his intention to make her ask for his help, to need him

just once, but his curiosity got the better of him and, more interested in her urgent desire to examine the contents of an old trunk
than in scoring points, he stood back and, inviting her to lead the
way, said, 'Shall we go?'

Neither of them moved, both remembering the last time he'd
said those words.

Then, abruptly, Sylvie said, 'There's really no need to bother
yourself.' Which did nothing to allay his curiosity. 'Honestly. I
know the way.'

'I'm sure you do, Sylvie, but it's no bother,' he assured her.
'I'm going to have to clear the attics very shortly and it will be
useful to have someone who can tell me what, exactly, is up there
before it gets tossed into a skip.'

'You wouldn't!' she declared, her eyes widening in a flash of
anger. So Miss Sylvie Duchamp Smith wasn't quite as detached
about her family's belongings—even the ones left to rot in the
attics—as she would have him believe.

'I might,' he said carelessly. 'One family's treasures are
another man's junk.'

'No doubt,' she said, that quick flash of fire back under control.

'Unless you can prove me wrong.'

'It's your junk. You must do with it as you wish.'

'True.' But having her acknowledge that fact gave him rather
less pleasure than he'd anticipated which was, perhaps, why he
said, 'I should warn you that it's pretty dusty up there so you
might want to change your shoes. It would be a pity to spoil them.'

'What?' She looked down, let slip a word that somehow didn't
sound quite as shocking when spoken in those crisp consonants,
perfectly rounded vowels.

'Is there a problem?' he enquired.

'Yes!' Then she wiggled her toes and, with an unexpected smile
that turned the silvery-blue to the colour of a summer sky, she

looked up and added, 'And, then again, no. It just means that, having worn them most of the morning, I'm going to have to buy them.'

'Is that a problem?' he asked, recalling Pam's earlier comments on the subject. 'I understood shoe-buying was the antidote to all feminine ills.'

'You shouldn't believe everything that Candy told you,' she snapped. 'And I'm not here for recreational shopping.'

'No?' Obviously wedding planning was her livelihood but, even so, he'd have thought she'd have been a little less matter-of-fact about it. 'I thought that was what weddings were invented for.'

'If you believe that, Tom, I suggest you familiarise yourself with the words of the marriage service,' Sylvie said, regarding him with a long cool look that made him wish he'd kept his mouth shut. Then, with an unexpected blush, she shook her head and said, 'The truth is that this wedding is more about recreational borrowing. But once you've worn the shoes, they're yours.'

'You'll never regret it,' he said, finding it easier to look at her feet than her face.

'I will if I don't change them. Why don't you go on and I'll catch you up?' she suggested, losing the tigerish protectiveness she'd shown when she'd thought he was prepared to throw the contents of all those trunks away. That touch of hauteur when she'd chastised him for his lack of respect for the marriage service. Instead, snapping back into a defensive attitude as she turned and walked quickly away, not waiting for him to answer her.

He did anyway, murmuring, 'No hurry,' as, for the second time that morning, he watched her retreat as fast as her pretty purple shoes would carry her. 'I might get lost.'

Too late. He already was.

CHAPTER SEVEN

SYLVIE took a few moments to splash water on her face. Regain her composure.

She shouldn't have asked him. She'd promised, but she had to be sure. She didn't want to believe him so incapable of feeling…

She blew her nose, tucked a wayward strand of hair back into her scarf. Regarded her reflection in the glass. 'Serves you right, my girl,' she said, then laid her hand against her waist. 'Be thankful for what you've got.'

And with that she changed into sensible shoes and rejoined Tom McFarlane at the foot of the stairs. Neither of them spoke but she was intensely conscious of him at her side, then at her back as she led the way up the last flight of narrow stairs to the attics.

Why on earth had he waited?

It wasn't as if he didn't know the way…

She reached for the light switch but he was a fraction faster and, as their hands connected, her mind was filled with the image of long fingers holding his pen, ticking off invoice after invoice, on that endless afternoon. The memory of their strength as he'd lifted her down from the van, the way they'd felt against her skin.

Demanding, tormenting, sensitive…

'I've got it,' he said pointedly and she yanked her hand back as if stung.

The tension between them was drawn so tight that she half expected the bulb to blow as he switched it on, but only the dust burned as, throwing a dim glow over the abandoned detritus of generations of Duchamp lives, it began to heat up.

'Good grief!' she said, more as a distraction than a genuine exclamation of surprise as she glanced around. 'What a mess!'

'I thought that was the general rule with attics? That they were a dumping ground?'

'Well, yes, but it helps if it's an ordered dumping ground.' Which it had been, mostly, and she'd hoped to be able to go straight to her grandmother's chest, grab the dress and run.

No matter what he'd said, or what she'd promised, she knew that spending any time up here picking over family history with Tom McFarlane would only underline the painful truth that he did not want to be part of it.

She'd asked him outright and he couldn't have made it plainer that he didn't want to know. Fine. Her only concern had been that he should know that he was about to become a father so that he could make a choice.

Well, he'd made it.

The last thing she wanted in her little girl's life was a father who didn't care about her. Better to stick with the myth of the sperm 'donor'. At least that way she would know she was totally wanted by her mother. Could believe that she had been planned. A joy.

That was real enough.

All she wanted to do now was get this *Celebrity* feature over and done with so that she could leave Longbourne Court and Tom McFarlane behind. Especially Tom McFarlane.

He was not good for her peace of mind under any circumstances and up here, alone, under the eaves with the belongings of generations of her family, the feeling was oddly intensified because, whether he wanted to be or not, he *was* part of it now, part of her family, no matter how much he despised them all.

'The trunks used to be lined up around the room so that you could get at them,' she explained, doing her best to keep this businesslike. 'Tidily.'

Looking around, it was obvious that things had been moved about in the recent past. Long enough ago for dust to have covered the clean spaces, but months rather than years.

'I imagine any number of surveyors have moved them over the years so that they could check out the fabric of the roof,' Tom said.

That it was an eminently reasonable suggestion did not make her feel any better.

'Yours being the latest, no doubt,' she snapped. 'Well, they should have jolly well put them back where they found them.'

'Maybe this *is* where they found them,' he pointed out, 'but I'll be sure to pass on your criticism.'

'Well…good,' she replied, lifting the lid of the trunk nearest to her, as if satisfied. Then reeled back.

'Good grief, what's that smell?'

'Camphor,' she said, flapping at the air to disperse the fumes, but only succeeding in stirring up the dust and making things worse. 'To keep away the moths,' she said, choking from the combination, 'which would otherwise have feasted…' she gasped for air '…on all this fine wool suiting.'

'And not just the moths. That smell would keep away anybody who ever thought about wearing them,' he assured her. Then, with concern, 'Are you all right? Is this okay? It won't affect the…'

The word didn't make it out of his mouth.

'Baby,' she snapped, still coughing. 'It's not a dirty word.'

'No. I'm sorry.'

'So you said.' If he'd been any stiffer he'd have cracked in two, she thought. 'But I'm not, so that's okay, isn't it?'

He closed the trunk. 'I'm happy for you,' he said, turning away to open a second trunk.

That was it? She thought the camphor had made her gasp but his carelessness left her mouthing the air like a fish out of water.

Could he really be so…indifferent?

'This is better,' he said as, with a complete lack of concern, he held out an old tinplate truck for her to see. The kind of toy that might have belonged to one of the youths in the photograph and was now worth a considerable amount of money. Then he picked up a teddy bear, dressed as a clown, which was worth a great deal more. He offered it to her. 'You'd have been better to have left your clothes behind and taken this.'

'Chance would have been a fine thing,' she said, taking it from him, feeling for the button in the ear.

Even the vintage wedding dress had been part of the estate according to the emotionless men who'd moved in to make an inventory of contents, watching her like hawks to make sure she didn't pack anything more valuable than her underwear. They'd actually taken apart the framed photograph of her mother before she'd packed it, just to be sure that nothing valuable was secreted behind the picture.

She hadn't argued with them. She'd been beyond making a scene, couldn't even be bothered to put the photograph back in the frame, but had abandoned that along with the rest of her life.

What did a picture frame matter? Or an old wedding dress, for that matter, when her groom had put the ceremony on hold until everything had been 'sorted out'. As if it ever could be.

What on earth was she doing up here looking for it now? This wasn't moving on. This was just wallowing in the past. Something you did when you had no future. She was carrying her future in her womb. His future too.

'It's definitely a Steiff,' she said, handing it back to him. 'And, because it's been shut away, the colours haven't faded, which will increase the value. I'd advise you to be very careful before you toss any of this stuff into a skip. Who knows, on a good day at auction, you might even recoup the cost of your wedding. Wouldn't that be ironic?' she pushed, desperate for a reaction of any kind.

The only indication that he'd heard was the slightest tightening of his jaw as he turned away from her.

'Is this what you're looking for?' he asked after opening another trunk to reveal more clothes, this time layered in tissue. Then, 'No camphor?' He glanced across at her. 'Don't moths attack women's clothes?'

Sylvie sighed and let it go, looking across at the chest Tom had opened. 'That's a sandalwood chest,' she said, wriggling between a couple of battered trunks to squeeze into the tiny space beside him without touching him. 'Natural moth proofing.'

Her attempt at avoidance was brought to naught by the fact that her centre of gravity had shifted and, despite the sensible shoes, she wobbled against him. In an instant his hand was around what had once been her waist and he was holding her safe. Just as he had once before.

For a moment their gazes seemed to lock, all breathing to cease, and it was that moment in the garage all over again.

'Okay?' he asked softly; his eyes in the dim light seemed to be dulled with anguish. It was just her imagination, she told herself. Or the dust…

She forced herself to turn away, look at the trunk, the dress, lying in its layers of snowy tissue.

'Oh…' Then, 'Yes…'

And the dust—or something—caught in her throat as she lifted her hand first to her lips, then out to touch the tissue paper. Curling her fingers back when she saw the state of them.

'What is it?' he asked.

'It's, um, just a dress…'

She'd wrapped it in tissue and returned it to the chest that contained her great-grandmother's clothes. The special ones. The ones she couldn't bear to part with. Designer gowns from Balenciaga, Worth, Chanel. Silk and velvet. Accessories from the art deco period. Bags, buckles, shoes. Even lingerie.

'My great-grandmother was very stylish. Very elegant. A bit of a trend-setter in her day,' she said with forced brightness. She must not cry. They were just things… 'They should have gone to the Melchester museum for their costume department. My mother had it on her list of things to do.' She blinked. No tears… 'You always think there's so much time…' Then, not wanting to think about that, she turned to him. 'What happened to your family?'

It was hard to say which of them was more shocked. Tom McFarlane, that she'd had the temerity to ask the question. Or her, for having dared pose it.

'I have no family,' he said without expression.

'That's not true!' And her hands flew protectively to the child at her waist, as if to cover her ears.

Not any more.

And she wanted to reach out, take his hand and place it on their growing child so that he could feel what it meant. Would understand.

'That's the way I like it,' he said, his expression so forbidding that, instead, she flinched. And then, before she could gather herself, speak, he gestured towards the tissue-wrapped dress in a manner that made it plain that the matter was closed.

'What's so special about this dress?'

After a long silence she turned to the trunk and, having rubbed her hands against the seat of her trousers to remove the dust, she unfolded the tissue to reveal the long lace veil.

Tom stared at the exquisite lace for a moment before turning to her and saying, 'Why am I surprised?' Then, 'Is this for your wedding?'

'Oh, please! I don't think the virginal veil is quite me, do you?' she asked, pulling a face, mocking herself. Mocking them both. Then, when he made no comment, 'Geena wanted to see it.' She shrugged. 'Embarrassing as it was, the visualisation exercise jarred loose some ideas and I think she has some thought of interpreting this dress for the new maturer, pregnant me. It won't do, of course.'

'Why don't you wait? Until after you've had the baby?'

'*Celebrity*'s copy date is fixed, I'm afraid. It's this weekend or never.' Then, looking up at him, 'Obviously they'll acknowledge that we've used it with your permission.'

'That really won't be necessary,' he replied. 'I've had more than enough of weddings to last me a lifetime. In fact, I'm beginning to feel as if I'm trapped in some nightmarish time-loop in which the word "wedding" is a constantly recurring theme.'

She finally snapped. 'Do you think you're the only one who's ever been stood up days before a wedding?' she demanded. 'Believe me, you'll get over it.'

'I have your guarantee?' Then, 'I'd forgotten. It happened to you too, didn't it?' And when, shocked, she didn't reply, 'I saw a piece about you in *Celebrity*.'

'Oh, that.' She shrugged. 'Yes, well, it was three weeks rather than three days in my case, but who's counting?'

'So tell me, Sylvie, how long did it take you to get over being left at the altar?'

'A great deal longer than you, Tom. Let's face it, you were over it the minute you put your hand up my skirt.'

The minute the words left her mouth, Sylvie regretted them. But she was angry with him, wanted to hurt him as he was hurting her. The pain that she'd felt as a nineteen-year-old, abandoned by the man she'd loved, was a world away from his hurt pride and she refused to indulge him in a session of mutual bonding over their shared experience of being dumped just before the wedding.

But, in her haste to deter his curiosity, she'd made a major mistake. Desperate to stop his thoughts—her thoughts—from dashing off in one direction, she had provoked another, equally powerful memory of that moment, inevitable as a lightning strike, when, compelled by some force outside all the norms of acceptable behaviour, they'd both totally lost it.

The searing heat of his mouth. An intimate and personal touch that had, in an instant, bypassed her will, overridden her mind, stolen everything. And, just for a moment, given her back something she'd thought lost for ever. Given her a lot more...

Equally powerful but without meaning, she reminded herself, even as his eyes seemed to darken, soften in response to the memories she'd so carelessly stirred up, as the electricity in the air raised the tiny hairs on her arms in a shiver of awareness.

She fought it, fought the need for his touch, her yearning for the soft whisper of words that she heard only in her dreams, knowing just how easy it would be to give in to the moment. Easy to say, but he was as close now as he had been then. Close enough that the scent of his wind-blown hair, newly laundered clothes, the faint musk of warm skin overrode the smell of camphor and hot dust.

Much too close.

Even in this dim light she knew her face would betray her thoughts, everything she was feeling, and he needed no more than the tiny betraying whimper of remembered joy, shatteringly loud, in the silence—an open invitation to repeat the experience, just in case his memory needed jogging—for his expression to change from thoughtful to something very different.

'Is that right?' he murmured, tightening his hold, bringing her round to face him so that his mouth was just inches from her own. 'Maybe we should try that again. So that you can explain it to me.'

Not in this world, she thought, but there was no time to object before his lips touched hers, sending a thrill of pleasure—the heat that haunted her dreams—spiralling through her.

'Step…' he said, his hand sliding beneath her long, loose top, cool against her warm skin as he leaned into her, deepening the kiss, and she shivered, but not with cold.

No…

This was wrong.

Stupid.

Inevitable.

Inevitable from the first moment he'd walked into her office. She'd known it. He'd known it. Like iron filings to a magnet. Why else would he—would she—have gone to such lengths to avoid each other? It was the only wedding she'd ever coordinated where the groom had been totally absent.

But inevitable didn't make it—

His tongue stroked her lower lip and every cell in her body responded as if to some unheard command, as if standing on tiptoe, reaching out for more.

'By…'

—right.

'Step…'

Oh… Confetti…

Her knees were water. Another minute and she'd be sprawled over one of the trunks in a rerun of that moment when that instant attraction had overcome every particle of common sense, every lesson that she'd ever learned about the fickleness of the human heart. When the heat had overcome the ice and turned it to steam.

To be overwhelmed, to forget yourself so completely might be excusable once.

Twice…

Her head felt like lead, she didn't have the strength to move it, break contact, but then his hand slid forward on its inevitable journey towards her breast and instead encountered the mound of her belly and, as if drawn to him, her baby girl turned, reached out to him. And he was the one whose head went back as if struck.

For a moment his expression was desolate, empty, but then as if, all along, it had been no more than a demonstration that she was still in his power, his to take or leave as he pleased, he let his hand drop to his side.

'Perhaps not,' he said, but with a touch of self-mockery. She didn't doubt that, as for her, the desire had been real enough, but maybe one of the reasons he was a billionaire was his ability to learn from past mistakes and never repeat them.

'Definitely not,' she said, although her mouth was dry, her voice woolly and not quite as steady as she intended. But, with the help of a steadying breath, she slowly jacked her self-control back into position. 'You don't need a step-by-step instruction manual, Tom McFarlane. You know all the moves.'

'Now, why,' he asked, looking down at her, 'do I get the impression that was not a compliment?'

'I'm sorry, but I really can't help you there,' she said as, with extreme care and ignoring the cold emptiness where for a moment his hand had rested against his growing child, she turned away and scooped up the tissue-wrapped gown, holding it across her arms in front of her. A shield. 'You're just going to have to work that one out for yourself.'

She managed a smile. If she managed to keep it light, to laugh it off as if it were nothing, staying on at Longbourne Court might, just might, be possible for the next few days.

And, pitifully, she didn't want to leave. Not yet. She'd fled in misery ten years earlier. This felt like a second chance to say goodbye properly.

And she hadn't quite given up on her baby's father.

His reaction to the baby's movement beneath his hand suggested he wasn't as immune to the idea of fatherhood as he thought. Maybe if she could somehow make him believe that she did not want anything for herself—convincing herself would be something else—he might find it in his heart to love a daughter, no matter how unexpected.

But not now. Not here. Right now, the only thing on her mind was to put some safe distance between them. Try to recover the little ground she seemed to have made when they'd been in the library.

'If you'll excuse me, I really must get this to Geena,' she said.

'The wedding must come first?'

And she thought she could do irony...

'The wedding *feature* must come first, Tom.' Then, 'Purple shoes. Purple waistcoats. I suspect Geena is already working on yours.'

'You're really going to wear them?' he said, refusing to be drawn in by the waistcoat. 'The shoes.'

'The idea is growing on me,' she admitted. 'What do you think?'

'I think it's the groom's job to colour coordinate with the bride. I also seem to recall that you promised to help me sort out the contents of the attics—'

'I will—'

'—but it seems that now you've found what you wanted you can't wait to escape.'

His tone was disparaging but she smiled nevertheless. His first reaction on seeing her had been to warn her not to get too comfortable. Now he was asking for her help, even though they both knew that auction houses would be falling over themselves for the chance to make an inventory of the contents of the Duchamp attics.

'Actually,' she replied, 'I think the deal was that I'd point out what was up here, but even that's going to take more than half an hour, which is just about all I've got right now.' Then, glancing around because it was safer than looking at him, 'What will you do with it all?'

'Is it any of your business?' he asked, reclaiming a little of the distance he'd briefly surrendered. 'Since it's all mine?'

It was in the nature of a challenge but she didn't rise to it. She'd ceased to think of any of this as hers a long time ago. 'No,' she said, shaking her head. Then, after a moment, 'None at all.'

'You don't mean that,' he said, regarding her through narrowed eyes. 'You want something. The bear? Your grandmother's clothes for the costume museum?'

Was he really capable of tempting her simply for his amusement? Or was his conscience beginning to prick him? There really was no need for him to feel bad about becoming the unwitting owner of the junk her family had stuffed up here.

'Actually, I'd quite like some of them for myself, but that's just self-indulgence,' she assured him.

Some things were lost for ever and you just had to accept it. Live with it.

'Why don't you just leave it all up here?' she suggested.

He shook his head. 'I need the room. Come on, you might as well tell me.'

She looked at him. He seemed serious enough and nothing ventured, nothing gained—she might as well ask for something that could be auctioned off to help the women her mother had cared so much about.

'Nothing for me. Truly. But if you're feeling generous, and since you thought it was all going to be rubbish anyway, maybe you'd consider giving a few things to help raise money for the Pink Ribbon Club?'

Tom McFarlane didn't know what he'd expected. But, surrounded by family treasures that she'd lost, given the opportunity to reclaim some precious memory, it had never occurred to him that she'd ask for something to give away.

'The charity your mother founded? What does it do, actually?'

'It supports women with cancer. And their families. When my mother was going through her treatment, she realised just how fortunate she was.'

'Private treatment? No waiting?'

'Cancer is like war, Tom. There are officers and there are men, but the bullets don't distinguish between them.'

'I'm sorry. That was a cheap shot.'

'Yes, actually, it was.' Then she lifted her shoulders in a barely-there shrug. 'But you're right. She had her chemo in a private room. Had the very best medical attention, every chance to recover. The thing was, Tom, she didn't take it for granted. She knew how lucky she was, which is why she took so much pleasure in being able to give something back.'

'But she still died.'

Pam had attempted to fill him in on some of the background while he'd had breakfast. He'd shut it out, concentrating on what had been happening with various projects he'd left in her more than capable hands when he'd taken to the hills, not on Sylvie Smith's family. But he had picked up the fact that Lady Annika Duchamp Smith was dead.

'Not from cancer. She was driving to London to talk to the bank in an attempt to sort out the mess.' Her gesture took in the attic, but that wasn't the mess she was referring to. 'The weather was bad, she was upset. I should have been with her instead of behaving like a bratty teenager.'

He saw her throat move as she swallowed and it was all he could do to stop himself from reaching out to her, but this time in a gesture of comfort.

Before he could make a total fool of himself—she'd finally got the Earl to provide her with every possible comfort—she gathered herself and said, 'Look, don't worry about it. You've loaned us the house. That's more than generous.' She didn't wait for an answer, but said, 'I have to go.'

'Or course. I mustn't delay you.'

With a wedding to plan and a baby on the way, she had more than enough to keep her occupied.

It wasn't a problem. He'd get someone from one of the auction houses to come and sort through the trunks. Put aside anything of value.

She paused in the doorway, looked back. 'If you like, I'll give you a hand later. If you're planning on staying?'

Was there just a hint of hope in her voice? A fervent wish that he'd make himself scarce and leave her to have the free run of the house, to be cosseted by the old family retainers for a few days so that she could pretend that nothing had changed?

Or was she expecting company?

'I'm staying,' he assured her, crushing it. Then regretted the thought.

Despite their similar backgrounds, she was nothing like Candy, who, it had to be admitted, was shallower than an August puddle.

No doubt she just wanted to forget, wipe from her memory, the moment when she'd clung, whimpering and pleading, to him. And who could blame her for that? Why on earth would she want to remember?

'Maybe, if you have some time to spare later, you could give me some clues as to what I might find,' he suggested.

'Well, there's nothing on television,' she said, 'so you've got yourself a date.' Then, almost as an afterthought, 'But do bring a brighter light bulb so that we can at least see what we're doing.'

She had that natural authority that would have had the serfs leaping to her bidding, he thought. Perfect lady of the manor material. And a smile that would have made them happy to leap.

If he wasn't careful, he'd find himself leaping right along with them.

'I'll ask Mr Kennedy to replace it,' he replied.

Just to make the point, in case she was in danger of forgetting, that this was *his* house and if anyone was going to issue orders in it it would be him.

CHAPTER EIGHT

SYLVIE watched with a certain amount of detachment as Geena and her staff went into raptures over her great-grandmother's wedding dress.

'This is so beautiful, Sylvie!' Geena said, examining the lace. The workmanship. 'French couturier?'

'Undoubtedly,' she said. 'Great-grandma Clementine started out as she meant to go on. But it's a dress for a very young bride. She was barely nineteen when she married my great-grandfather.'

She managed a shrug, as if such a thing was unbelievable.

'I agree. I've designed something much more sophisticated for you. Flowing, loose, since it's a style that suits you so well. No veil, though. I thought a loose-fitting jacket with wide sleeves, turned-back cuffs.'

She proffered her sketches.

Sylvie swallowed. 'It's absolutely gorgeous, Geena. Perfect. What's that in my hair?'

'A small tiara. Nothing over the top,' she added with a grin. 'Since you seem hooked on elegant restraint.'

'I don't know about restraint,' Sylvie said with a wry smile. 'There are the purple shoes.' She gave a little shrug. 'I forgot I was wearing them so I had to buy them.'

'If you believe that, my darling, who am I to contradict you? I'll put in an order for the purple waistcoat then, shall I?'

'Will anything I say stop you?'

'I don't know, give it a try.'

She shook her head.

'Okay, you can leave the tiara to me, if you like. The woman who makes them for me is showing at the Fayre. Can we add a touch of green to the violet? You're not superstitious?'

'No.' She'd done everything by the book the first time and it had still all fallen apart. And this time it was make-believe, so it really didn't matter. 'I'll send you over a colour sample—'

'Don't worry, I'll pick it up when I come over with my final drawings and material swatches for the appliqué first thing in the morning. Be ready to make a decision.'

'I've got the message, but now I really have to love you and leave you because I have an appointment with the caterer, the florist and the confectioner.'

Followed by an evening cosseted with the devil himself, sorting through the discarded ephemera of generations of the Duchamp family.

Not the brightest of decisions, considering the effect he had upon her. She couldn't think what had made her volunteer. Or maybe she could, which was truly dumb, even though he hadn't carried through with this morning's opportunistic pass. Despite the fact that she hadn't done a single thing to discourage him.

Somehow they'd managed to move on without sinking into terminal embarrassment, although only she knew how hard it had been to keep it light, make a joke of it.

Only she knew how torn she was between relief and regret that he'd taken a step back, rescuing her from her runaway hormones.

She might have spent the last six months yearning for the phone to ring, for him to make a move, to suggest they continue where they'd left off, but the truth was that some affairs were doomed from the start. And that was all it would ever have been for him—a tit-for-tat affair to throw oil on the fire of gossip and give him back his pride.

A lesser man would have gone for it without a second thought. Used it to bolster his shattered self-esteem. Used her to strike back.

That he hadn't seemed to prove that Tom McFarlane was made of finer stuff. He didn't need to hurt someone else to make himself feel good. Not even her, even though he couldn't have made it plainer that he despised everything that made her who she was. A reaction which only increased her curiosity about the forces that had shaped his character.

She frowned as she wondered about his lack of family memories.

His meteoric rise from teenage entrepreneur to billionaire was the stuff of legend, but where had that teenager risen from? If he had no family, it would go a long way to explaining his inability to confront emotional issues. His coldness in the face of Candy's desertion. His inability to connect physical love with anything deeper.

Maybe.

But it would have to keep, she told herself with a sigh as she pulled into the caterer's premises, trying to raise her enthusiasm for the latest twist on poached salmon—never a favourite.

'Something smells good,' Sylvie said as she tossed a folder containing menus, photographs of flowers and every style of cake imaginable on to the kitchen table and crossing to the stove where Tom, unbelievably, was beating potato into submission. 'Mrs Kennedy's spiced beef casserole?'

'It's beef and it's a casserole, beyond that I'm not prepared to hazard a guess,' Tom said. 'I'm only responsible for the vegetables.'

He offered her the pan and Sylvie dipped a finger in the

potatoes, licked it and groaned with pleasure. 'Butter, garlic. Real food.'

'There's plenty for two,' he said, apparently amused at her pleasure.

'Are you sure? I'd better warn you that I'm starving.'

'A first. A woman with an appetite,' he said, his smile fading as quickly as it had come. 'But then you're eating for two.'

'Oh, I've never been a fan of lettuce,' she said, too hungry to worry about his sudden loss of interest, instead reaching up to the warming rack above the stove for a couple of plates. 'Where's Mrs Kennedy?' she asked. 'Why isn't she mashing your spuds?'

'She's putting her feet up after being run ragged by the hordes of exhibitors and construction people tramping through the house all day, wanting tea, scones and sandwiches. You are aware that they're eating us out of house and home?'

Us?

Just a figure of speech, no doubt, but it sent a thrill of pleasure rippling through her tired limbs.

'Send the bill to *Celebrity;* this is their party,' she replied and, since emotion was off his radar, doing her best to keep the smile down and the tone chirpy.

'They're picking up the tab for everything?' he asked, glancing at her.

'Peanuts for them. You missed out, Tom. If you'd let them cover your wedding they'd have been stuck with the bill.'

'And filled their pages with the story when Candy made her break. No, thanks. It was enough of a circus already.'

Sylvie grinned. 'You got off lightly, Tom. Last month I orga-nised a wedding where the bride arrived on an elephant—'

'Stop! Stop right there.'

'And you escaped the butterflies…'

'Give me a break,' he said, but he was grinning too.

'Okay. But only because you're being so protective of Mrs Kennedy. Although I bet she had a whale of time with an endless stream of people to fuss over for a change.'

'A stream of people taking advantage.'

'Rubbish. She didn't *have* to make scones. She didn't have to offer them anything. The workmen almost certainly brought flasks and packed lunches with them.'

Tom's only response was a noise that sounded like something a disgruntled bulldog might have made as he spooned some of the rich casserole on to a plate.

'I understood the Fayre was your party,' he said. 'Pink ribbons and all.'

'Okay,' she said, opening a drawer and finding knives and forks for both of them, before pulling out a chair and making herself comfortable at the kitchen table. 'Why don't you send the bill to me and *I'll* send it on to *Celebrity?*' Then, 'And I promise that I won't make you go through it item by item.'

'No?' he said as he put his own plate on the table, holding her attention while he fetched two glasses and a bottle of red wine that was already open. Then, as he looked up and caught her gaze, 'Maybe I'll insist.'

And Sylvie blushed. What an idiot! Anyone would think she was angling for a repeat performance…

Maybe she was.

'But tomorrow they're on their own,' he continued as he pulled out a chair and sat down opposite her.

She cleared her throat. 'Right.' Then, 'Will you tell Mrs Kennedy that you're going to spoil her fun? Or would you like me to do that?'

He shook his head, trying not to smile. 'Just tell her not to overdo it. Meantime,' he said, 'I don't expect her to wait on me.'

'Perish the thought,' she agreed as he filled both glasses

without bothering to ask her whether she wanted wine or not and he looked up, apparently catching the ironic tone.

'What?'

She shrugged. 'Well, I may be wrong,' she said, getting up and fetching a bottle of water from the fridge and another glass, 'but I suspect she's disappointed not to have had the chance to lay out everything in the dining room to show the new "master" what she can do.' Then, as he scowled, presumably at falling into her trap, 'And maybe just a little anxious about their future too. They have a pension—that was ring-fenced—but their cottage has been their home for thirty years.'

'I don't suppose anyone was worrying about that when the bailiffs were in.'

'You suppose wrong. My mother was deeply concerned. As far as she was concerned, they had tenure for life and it was one of the things she hoped to straighten out.' She dismissed that. It was past. 'I'm not trying to get at you, Tom. I'm just telling you how it is.'

For a moment he just stared at her, then he nodded. 'I'll give it some thought.'

'Thank you.' Then, 'Where's Pam tonight? Isn't she hungry?'

'She's taken the opportunity, with my presence, to go back to London for a couple of days to catch up.' He raised an ironic glass in her direction. 'It's just you, me and the ghosts.'

Okay, maybe she'd asked for that with her 'master' crack. He couldn't have made it clearer that he despised the landed gentry and everything they stood for.

Would no doubt enjoy turning this venerable old manor house into a conference centre, the stables into accommodation for bright young executives. Take pleasure in the thought of them being moulded into team leaders as they played paintball war games in the ancient woodland.

And why not?

It was a new era, meritocracy ruled and she should be using this opportunity to demonstrate her own company's experience in the field of conference coordination.

She'd relish the chance to expand her business in that direction.

Whatever Josie thought, she had, like Tom, had enough of weddings to last her a lifetime. And she was losing her taste for celebrity parties too. Maybe it was impending motherhood but she wanted to do something a little more grown-up and meaningful with the rest of her life than think of new ways to spend other people's money. When this week was over she was going to talk to Josie about a partnership, gift her the 'fun' side of the business so that she could concentrate on more serious stuff.

She didn't think that Tom McFarlane would be that impressed if she used the opportunity to pitch for his business, however, so she poured herself a glass of water and, matching his gesture, touched it to his.

'To the ghosts,' she said, 'although I have to warn you that they're all family. Protective of their own.' She swallowed a mouthful of water, put down her glass, then picked up a fork and speared a small piece of tender beef. 'I'll sleep soundly enough tonight,' she lied. How likely was that with him just yards away? 'You, on the other hand, are going to be tearing the place apart and I doubt they'll take kindly to that.'

'Then I'm glad you're here. If they come calling, I'll seek refuge with you.'

She choked as she swallowed the beef. Then, unable to help herself, laughed. 'Why on earth would I protect you?'

'Because this is all your fault.' He gestured around the kitchen with his fork. 'If you'd kept your staff under better control, Candy would have had her country estate and Longbourne Court would have been safe for another fifty years.'

She stared at him, shocked out of her teasing. Her appetite suddenly non-existent. 'You bought this for Candy?'

He didn't answer her question, but just said, 'Do you think she would have thought twice about running off with Quentin if she'd known?'

Sylvie lifted her shoulders and said, 'It was always Candy's declared ambition to marry a millionaire, Tom, and she came close more than once, as I'm sure you know.'

He shrugged. 'She could scarcely deny that there hadn't been a certain amount of history,' he admitted. 'Her romances were always given the full *Celebrity* treatment.'

'As were her break-ups. She had a habit of doing something outrageous, wrecking her chances.'

'So? What are you saying? That I'm the last in a long line to get her very individual style of brush-off?'

She shook her head. 'Not exactly.' She stirred the creamy potato with her fork. 'I always assumed it was because she thought she could do better. Had someone richer, more interesting, more exciting in her sights. But then she had you, Tom, and she still ran.'

The corners of his eyes fanned into a smile. 'I do believe you've just paid me a compliment.'

'I do believe I have,' she replied, matching his smile and raising it. Then, feeling slightly giddy, 'I've been thinking about it ever since I saw them together. When they came home.' The change in her had been extraordinary. 'She didn't leave you for someone richer or more interesting, but for sweet, adorable Quentin. A man without anything very much to offer her except love.'

'And the prospect of a title.'

'He comes from long-lived stock, Tom. No one inherits in that family until they're drawing their pension.'

'Then why?'

'Why did she marry him? I guess she finally found what she'd been looking for all this time. The missing ingredient.'

Tom frowned.

'They were in love,' she said. 'I'm sorry, but hearts trumps diamonds. Love trumps everything.'

'I'm glad for her.' Maybe she didn't look convinced, because he said, 'Truly. We both had what the other wanted, or in her case thought she wanted. But neither of us was ever so lost to reality that we believed we were in love.'

'Reality is a good basis for marriage,' Sylvie assured him, moved at his unexpected generosity. 'There's so much less possibility of disillusion setting in over the honeymoon cornflakes.'

She'd seen the mess that friends—'deeply in love' friends— had made of their marriages.

'It's a great theory but it doesn't take account of the X factor that makes fools of us all.' Then, 'You didn't answer my question.'

'Would Longbourne Court have been enough to carry Candy up the aisle?' She regarded him thoughtfully. 'Do you regret not telling her?'

'There's no right answer to that question.'

'No, but if it helps, I've known Candy since we were both twelve years old and I've never seen her so…*involved.* For what it's worth, I don't think the crown jewels would have swayed her.'

'In that case, I'm glad I didn't tell her.' He clearly didn't have quite the same faith in the power of 'the real thing' as she did. Then, obviously not wanting to pursue the matter, he said, 'How are your wedding plans coming along? Did the dress do the trick?'

'Geena is happy,' she said, not elaborating.

'What about you?'

She lifted her shoulders. 'It's her show and I'm sure the result will be stunning. To be honest, I'm getting to the point where I just want the whole thing over with.'

Tom regarded her steadily. 'Isn't this supposed to be the happiest day of a woman's life? Every fantasy she ever dreamed of?'

'Yes, well, right now, Tom, my fantasy would be to have someone else arranging all the details. I suddenly see the attraction of hiring a wedding planner; I really should have left this to my assistant.' Josie would have been great. 'Unfortunately, she's already handling both our jobs.'

Tom regarded Sylvie with a touch of real concern. There were dark hollows beneath her eyes, at her temples and, despite her assertion that she was starving, she was doing little more than push her food around the plate.

This was all too much for her.

She should be resting, not racing about trying to organise a wedding at a moment's notice when she had a demanding job, a company to run. Where the devil was her 'groom'? The father of her baby? Why wasn't he taking on some of the burden of this?

'If you don't mind me saying so, Sylvie, you don't appear to be enjoying this very much.'

'Believe me, only the fact that I'm supporting a very worthwhile charity induced me to put myself through this.'

He frowned. There was something not quite right about all this, but he couldn't put his finger on it. 'How much did *Celebrity* offer to cover this wedding of yours?'

'Nowhere near enough,' she said, finally breaking into a laugh. 'It doesn't help that it's all at such short notice.' He was staring at her. 'Because of the Wedding Fayre?' she prompted.

Was that it?

Did her Earl, so recently freed from one marriage, think he was being rushed, pressured into another, not just by her pregnancy but to support her charity?

It would take a brave man to ask a soon-to-be bride that particular question and he confined himself to, 'Above and beyond the call of duty, no doubt, but with your experience it must be little more than going through the motions.'

She sighed. 'You'd think so, wouldn't you?' she said, toying with the mash so that he wanted to scoop it up, forkful by forkful, and feed it to her in small comforting bites. 'I've done it hundreds of times for other people. The problem is that I have a reputation to maintain. My "wedding" has got to have that special wow factor,' she said, looking about as 'wowed' as a post-party balloon. 'It's got to be imaginative, different, original.'

'So what's the problem?'

'I need a theme. Normally I have a bride to drive that enthusiasm, feed me with ideas. Too many ideas, sometimes.'

'And you don't have any ideas about what you want for your own wedding?'

'Sad, isn't it?' she said, pulling a face. 'The problem is that I've done all this before. Spent months planning every last detail.'

'Not everyone gets a second chance to get it right.'

'Maybe that's the problem. It was perfect the first time.' She smiled a little sadly. 'Too perfect. I drive Josie crazy demanding she find some tiny flaw, something that went wrong…'

'The Arabs weave tiny mistakes into their carpets in the belief that only God can make things perfect.'

She looked at him, her eyes lit up. 'That's it. That's exactly it… When Jeremy was five and I was in my cradle, our families were already planning a dynastic marriage and like well-behaved children we did the decent thing and fell in love.'

'How convenient.'

'You think we were just talked into it?' she asked, less than amused. 'In love with the idea?'

'I may think that but I wouldn't dare make the mistake of saying so,' Tom hurriedly assured her.

'Of course you would. You just did. But honestly, it couldn't have been more perfect. Then my grandfather died, the creditors moved in and the wedding was put on hold.'

Then her mother had died too. While she was behaving like a bratty teen because she'd been dumped by the man she'd loved—his entire family—because they didn't want to be connected to the disaster.

'And Jeremy?' he asked. 'What happened to him?' Because something evidently had.

'Oh, he was offered a transfer abroad by his company.'

'That would be Hillyer's Bank?'

'It would.'

'Convenient. I imagine he was shipped out of harm's way so that the relationship could die a natural death.'

'Cynic.'

'But right.'

Money and land marrying money and land. He suspected that the only one who had been totally innocent was Sylvie—much too young to cope with a world of hurt. Without thinking, he reached out and wrapped his fingers around hers.

Startled, she looked up and he saw her swallow, blink back tears that she'd let flow in the aftermath of lovemaking. And, just as he had been then, he was overwhelmed with a sense of helplessness. 'I'm sorry, Sylvie,' he said, removing his hand from hers, picking up his glass, although he didn't drink from it.

'Don't be.'

No. She'd got her happy ending. Ten years late, but it had all come right in the end for her. So why were her eyes still shining with unshed tears?

How many had she wasted already on a man who was so clearly not worth a single one?

'Marriage is for better or worse and we were far too young, too immature, to handle the "worse",' she said, as if she had to explain. 'At least this way we didn't become just another statistic.'

'There's an up side to everything,' he said. 'So they say.' Even the cruellest wounds scarred over with time and Jeremy Hillyer, newly elevated to his earldom, had finally returned to claim his childhood sweetheart. And, before he could stop himself, Tom found himself saying, 'Is there anything I can do to help?'

'Excuse me?'

She might well look surprised. He'd hardly been the most welcoming of hosts.

But then, having always considered love to be just another four-letter word, he appeared to have been sideswiped by feelings that wouldn't go away. That just got deeper, more intense the more he'd tried to evade them.

It seemed that the man with a reputation for never letting an opportunity slip his grasp had, in the biggest deal of his life, missed his chance.

'With the wedding?' he said.

'You're kidding?' And, out of the blue, she laughed. A full-bodied, joyful laugh that lit up her eyes as the sun lit the summer sky. Then, 'Oh, right, I get it. You think if you can hurry things along I'll be out of your hair all the quicker.'

'You've got me,' he said, even though it had, in fact, been the furthest thing from his mind. Sitting here with her, sharing a meal, talking about nothing very much, was an experience he thought he would be happy to repeat three times a day for the rest of his life.

Well, that was never going to happen. But he had today, this week and, despite everything, he found that he was laughing too.

'So? The dress—' and she'd wanted an updated version of the original dress, he now realized '— is taken care of. What's next?'

She looked confused, uncertain, as well she might.

'It's therapy,' he assured her. 'Confronting what you fear most.'

'Oh, right.'

Was that disappointment? Not the explanation she'd been looking for? Hoping for?

'Food,' she said, accepting it. 'Something a man so wonderfully gifted with a potato masher must surely know all about.'

'A man who lives alone needs to know how to cook.'

'I wouldn't have thought that was a problem. Surely women are fighting over the chance to feed you, prove themselves worthy.'

'Not the kind of women I date,' he said.

And she blushed. He loved how she did that.

'This should be right up your street, then,' she said, ducking her head as she pushed the glossy menu brochure across the table to him. Then, holding on to it, she asked, 'What would be your perfect wedding breakfast?'

There had been something intense about the way she'd said that, about the look she gave him. As if there was some deeper meaning. As if she was trying to tell him something.

'Probably nothing in here,' he admitted, waiting—although what for he could not have said.

She shrugged as she finally released it. 'Surprise me.'

He picked it up, but couldn't take his eyes off her. She wasn't glamorous in the way that Candy had been glamorous. But she had some quality that called to him. A curious mixture of strength and vulnerability. She was a woman to match him, a woman he wanted to protect. A combination that both confused him and yet seemed to make everything seem so simple.

Except for the fact that she was carrying another man's child. A man who'd run out on her when she'd needed him most. And apparently had to do nothing more than turn up to pick up the threads and carry on as if nothing had happened.

'The deal is that I check out the menu, you eat,' he said.

For a moment he thought she was going to argue, but then she picked up her fork, using the food as a shield to disguise the fact that she was blushing again. Something she seemed to do all the time, even though she'd responded to him like a tiger. The woman was a paradox. One he couldn't begin to understand. Didn't even try. Just waited until he was sure that she was eating, rather than just pushing the food around her plate, before he gave his full attention to the simpler task of choosing a menu for her wedding, just as, twelve months ago, she'd been choosing one for his.

Sylvie, watching Tom flicking through the sample menus, rediscovered her appetite. Somehow, talking to him, she'd finally managed to bury every last remnant of the hurt that Jeremy had caused her.

Learning that he'd met someone else in America, was getting married, the arrival of each of his children, had been a repetition of the knife plunge to her heart, each as painful as that first wound inflicted on the day he'd told her that they needed 'a little space'. That he was going away for a while just when she'd needed him most.

Maybe if he hadn't been her first love, her only love, she'd have got over it sooner. As it was, no one had touched her until Tom McFarlane had walked into her office and, with just one look, had jump-started her back into life, just as the garage jump-started her car when the battery was flat.

There would be no more tears over Jeremy Hillyer. Tom McFarlane had erased every thought of him; she'd scarcely recognised him when he'd turned up at that reception. Not because he'd aged badly, far from it. But because it was so easy to see him for the shallow man he'd always been.

No more tears for the girl she'd been either.

They'd threatened for a moment, but Tom had been there and they'd dried off like a summer mist.

The trick now would be to avoid shedding any over him.

He looked up from the brochure and, with an expression of

disgust, said, 'Is this really what people are expected to eat at weddings? Fiddly bits of fish. Girl food. We've got to be able to do better than that.'

We. The word conjured up a rare warmth but she mustn't read too much into it. Or this.

'The idea is that it's supposed to look pretty on a plate,' she said.

'For *Celebrity* or for you?'

'Is there a difference?'

'Whose wedding is this?' he demanded, disgusted. 'What would you really choose? If you didn't have to pander to the whims of a gossip magazine?'

Whoa…Where had that come from? It wasn't just irritation, it was anger. As if it really mattered.

'They are paying a lot of money to have their whims pandered to,' she reminded him. 'Besides, there are the Wedding Fayre exhibitors to think of. This is their big chance.'

'It's your wedding. You should have what you want.'

That did make her laugh. 'If only, but I don't think ten minutes with the registrar in front of two witnesses, followed by a fish and chip supper would quite fill the "fantasy" bill, do you?'

'That's what you'd choose?'

'Quick, simple. Sounds good to me.' Then, because his expression was rather too thoughtful, 'That's classified information, by the way.'

'Of course. I realise how bad it would be for business if it got out that the number one wedding planner hated weddings.'

'I didn't say that!'

'Didn't you? Or are you saying that it's only your own wedding that you can't handle?'

'I can handle it!' Of course she could handle it. If she wasn't here. If he wasn't here. 'It's just that it's all been a bit of a rush. I can't seem to get a hold of it. Find my theme.'

'Why don't you wait until after the baby arrives? Isn't that what most celebrities do these days?'

'I'm not a celebrity,' she snapped. 'And the Wedding Fayre is this weekend.'

'There'll be other fayres.'

'People are relying on me, Tom, and when I make a commitment, I deliver. It's a done deal.'

'So you're going through this hoopla just for the sake of a donation to charity?'

'It's a really big donation, Tom. We'll be able to do so much with the money. And I really do want to help local businesses.'

'That's it?'

'Isn't it enough?'

'I thought we'd already agreed that it wasn't, but who am I to judge?' He sounded angry, which was really stupid. Her fault for making such a fuss, but before she could say so, apologise, he said, 'Fish and chips?'

'Out of the paper. Or sausage and mash. Something easy that you can eat with friends around the kitchen table.'

'Well, it certainly beats anything I've seen in here,' he agreed, tossing the menu brochure back on the pile of stuff she'd gathered during the afternoon. 'I didn't know there were so many ways of serving salmon.'

She groaned. 'I loathe salmon. It's just so…so…'

'Pink?' he offered, breaking the tension, and they both grinned.

'That's the word.' Then, 'Come on.' She stood up, began to gather the plates. 'Let's clear this away and then we'll go and take a look at the attics.'

'Forget the attics. Go and sit down. I'll bring you some coffee.'

She leaned back a little, pushed back a heavy strand of hair that had escaped the chiffon scarf and tucked it behind her ear. 'Excuse me?'

'You've been running around all day. You need to put your feet up. Rest.'

'Well, thanks for that, Tom. You've just made me feel about as attractive as a—'

'You *look* wonderful,' he said. 'In fact, you could be a poster girl for all those adjectives that people use when they describe pregnant women.'

'That would be fat.'

'Blooming.'

'Just another word for fat.'

'Glowing,' he said, putting his hands on the table and leaning forward. 'Apart from the dark smudges under your eyes that suggest you're not getting enough sleep.'

'Tired and fat. Could it be any worse?'

'Well,' he said, appearing to consider her question, 'maybe you're a little thinner about the face.'

About to protest, she caught the gleam in his eye and realised that he was teasing.

'Tired, fat and gaunt. Got it,' she said, but she couldn't keep the smile from her face. Teasing! Who would have thought it? 'You haven't mentioned the swollen ankles.'

'Your ankles are not swollen,' he said with the conviction of a man who paid close attention. Then, as if aware that he'd overstepped some unspoken boundary, 'Don't worry. I'm sure a skilled photographer will be able to produce pictures that won't give the game away.'

She groaned. 'The photographer. I forgot to call the photographer. It's true what they say. My brain is turning to Swiss cheese…'

'All the more reason for you to go and put your feet up now. The drawing room has been surrendered to your Wedding Fayre, but there's a fire in the library.'

'Mr Kennedy lit a fire? What bliss.'

'I lit a fire when I was working in there this afternoon. Go and enjoy it.'

'I will. Thank you.' That was the thing about living on your own. No one ever told you to put your feet up or brought you a cup of coffee. For a moment she couldn't think of anything to say. Then the word 'coffee' filtered through and she said, 'Not coffee. Tea. Camomile and honey. You'll find the tea bags—'

He closed the gap between them and kissed her, and she forgot all about tea bags.

It was a barely-there kiss.

A stop talking kiss.

The kind of kiss she could lean into and take anywhere she wanted and she knew just how right it would be because they'd done that before. But how wrong too. She wanted him just as much—more, because this time it would be her decision, one made with her heart, her head. Not just a response to that instinct to mate in times of stress that had overwhelmed them both.

But she wanted Tom involved with his baby. That was the important relationship here. Her desires were unimportant.

Maybe he understood that too, because he was the one who leaned back. Left a cold place where, for just a moment, it had been all warmth.

'—somewhere,' she finished, somehow managing to make that sound as if nothing had intervened between the first part of the sentence and its conclusion. Then, because keeping up that kind of pretence was never going to be possible, she quickly scooped up her laptop and the brochures and walked away.

Not that it helped. She could still feel his lips clinging to hers. Still feel the tingle of that kiss all the way to her toes.

CHAPTER NINE

FOR a whole minute Tom didn't move. Taking the time to regain control over his breathing, over parts of him that seemed to have a will of their own.

His heart, mainly.

For a moment there he'd been certain that Sylvie was going to kiss him back. Reach up, put her hands to his cheeks and hold him while she kissed him and he climbed over the table to get at her, show her everything he was feeling.

But this time she didn't lose it. Attuned to her in some way he didn't begin to understand, he'd sensed an almost imperceptible hesitation and he'd put a stop to it before he embarrassed himself, or her.

In fact common sense suggested that the most sensible thing he could do right now was walk out of the back door, climb into his car and head for the safety of London.

But he'd run before. There was no help for him in distance and Sylvie was locked into another relationship. She'd said it plainly enough. She'd made a commitment and she always delivered on her word.

No matter what she was feeling deep down, and he knew she had felt the same dark stirring of desire that had moved him, she wouldn't lose her head again.

As for him, the need to face himself in the mirror every morning would keep him from doing anything he'd regret. Hurting her any more than he already had.

He dragged both hands through his hair, flattening it to his head, staring at the ceiling as he let out a long, slow breath.

He'd lived without love so long that he could barely remember what it felt like, could only remember the fallout, the pain. It was an alien concept, something he could not begin to understand. And spending a lifetime watching from the sidelines as friends and acquaintances fell apart and put themselves back together again offered few clues. He had always kept his distance until, finally, he'd arranged what had seemed like the perfect marriage to the perfect trophy wife. A woman who'd neither given nor wanted deep emotional commitment.

Just the perfect trophy husband.

Then he'd come face to face with Sylvie Duchamp Smith and, from that moment on, his perfect marriage had hung like a millstone round his neck. But, like Sylvie, he'd made a commitment and, like her, he always delivered on his promises.

Yet even when he'd been granted a last-minute reprieve he'd still fought against feelings he did not understand. He'd been emotionally incapable of saying the words that would have made everything right. Had instead, for the second time in his life, reduced a woman to tears.

His punishment was to watch helplessly as she planned her wedding. A wedding that she didn't appear to be anticipating with any excitement, or pleasure, or joy.

He clung to the edge of the sink, reminding himself that she was pregnant. That whatever she was doing, for whatever reason, her baby had to come first.

He turned on the tap but, instead of filling the kettle, he

scooped up handfuls of water, burying his face in it to cool the heat of lips that still tasted of her.

And then, when that didn't help, ducking his head beneath the icy water.

Sylvie abandoned her burden on the library table and gave herself up to the comfort of one of the old leather wing-chairs pulled up by the fire and closed her eyes, but more in despair than pleasure.

The intensity of the attraction had not diminished, that much was obvious. It wasn't just her; it was a mutual connection, something beyond words, and yet it was as if there was an unseen barrier between them.

Or perhaps it was the all too visible one.

One of the things that Candy had been most happy about her 'arranged' marriage was the fact that Tom wasn't interested in children and her figure was safe for postperity.

But that was the thing about arranged marriages. There had to be something in it for both parties. This house was a pretty clear indication of what Tom had in mind. Posterity. An heir, and almost certainly a spare. Maybe two.

The family he'd never had.

So what was his problem?

If it was a business arrangement he wanted, she had the same class, connections, background as Candy and she was nowhere near as expensive. On the contrary, she was entirely self-supporting. And the heir was included.

Maybe it was her lack of silicone implants that was the deal-breaker, she thought, struggling against a yawn. Or the lack of sapphire-blue contact lenses.

'If that's what he wants, then I'm sorry, kid, we're on our own,' she murmured.

* * *

Tom pushed open the library door and stopped as he saw Sylvie stretched out in one of the fireside chairs, limbs relaxed, eyes closed, head propped against the broad wing.

Fast asleep, utterly defenceless and, in contrast to the hot desire he'd done his best to drown in a torrent of cold water, he was overwhelmed by a great rush of protectiveness that welled up in him.

Utterly different from anything he'd ever felt for anyone before.

Was that love?

How did you know?

As quietly as he could, so as not to disturb her, he placed the tray on a nearby table and then took the chair opposite her, content just to watch the gentle rise and fall of her breathing. Content to stay like that for ever.

But nothing was for ever and after a few minutes her eyelids flickered. He saw the moment of confusion as she surfaced, then the smile as she realised where she was.

A smile that faded when she saw him and, embarrassed at being caught sleeping, struggled to sit up. 'Oh, Lord, please tell me I wasn't drooling.'

'Hardly at all,' he reassured her, getting up and placing a cup on the table beside her. 'And you snore really quietly.'

'Really? At home the neighbours complain.'

'Oh, well, I was being kind…' He offered her a plate of some home-made biscuits he'd found as she laughed. Teasing her could be fun… 'Have one of these.'

'Mrs Kennedy's cure-alls? Who could resist?'

'Not me,' he said, taking one himself. Then, as it melted in his mouth, 'I can see how they got their name. Maybe she should market them? A whole rang of Longbourne Court Originals?'

'With a picture of the house on the wrapper? Perfect for the nostalgia market. Except, of course, that there won't be

Longbourne Court for much longer. Longbourne Conference Centre Originals doesn't have quite the same ring to it, does it?'

He didn't immediately answer. And, when he did, he didn't answer the question she'd asked.

'When you asked me if I bought the house for Candy, I may have left you with the wrong impression.'

The words just tumbled out. He hadn't known he was going to say them. Only that they were true.

'You always intended to convert it?'

'No!' He shook his head. 'No. I told myself I was buying it for her. The ultimate wedding present. But when I walked into the house, it was like walking into the dream I'd always had of what a family home should be like. There were old wax jackets hanging in the mud room. Wellington boots that looked as if somebody had just kicked them off. Every rug looked as if the dog had been sleeping there just a moment before.'

'And all the furniture in "country house" condition. In other words, tatty,' Sylvie said.

'Comfortable. Homely. Lived in.'

'It's certainly that.'

'Candy would have wanted to change everything, wouldn't she? Get some fancy designer in from London to rip it all out and start from scratch.'

'Probably. It scarcely matters now, does it?' She lifted a brow but, when he didn't respond, subsided back into the comfort of the chair. 'This is total bliss,' she said, nibbling on the biscuit. 'Every winter Sunday afternoon of childhood rolled into one.' Then, glancing at him, 'Is it raining?'

'Raining?'

'Your hair seems to be dripping down your collar.'

'Oh, that. It's nothing. I missed the kettle and the water squirted up at me,' he lied.

'And only got your hair?' That eyebrow was working over-time. 'How did you get so lucky? When that happens to me, I always get it full in the face and chest.'

'Well, as you've already noticed, I've got a damp collar, if that helps.'

'You think I'm that heartless? Come closer to the fire or you'll catch a chill.'

He didn't need a second invitation but took another biscuit and settled on the rug with his back propped up against the chair on the far side of the fireplace.

'Tell me about your winter Sundays, Sylvie.'

'I'd much rather hear about yours.'

'No, believe me, you wouldn't. They are definitely nothing to get nostalgic over.' Then, because he didn't even want to think about them, 'Come on. I want everything, from the brown bread and butter to three choices of cake.'

'We never had three choices of cake!' she declared in mock outrage. 'According to my mother, only spoilt children had three kinds of cake.'

'I'll bet you had toasted teacakes. Or was it muffins?'

'Crumpets. It was always crumpets,' she said, still resisting him. 'I will have your story.'

'You'll be sorry if you do.' But for just a moment he was tempted by something in her eyes. Tempted to unburden himself, share every painful moment. But he knew that, once he'd done that, she'd own him, he'd be tied to her for ever, while she belonged to someone else.

'Did you toast them on one of those long toasting forks in front of the fire?' he asked.

And, finally, she let it go with a laugh.

'Oh, right. I remember you, Tom McFarlane. You were the grubby urchin with your face pressed up against the window-pane.'

Her laughter was infectious. 'I wish, but I was running wild, scavenging in Docklands while you were still on training wheels. But if I had been standing at the window, you'd have invited me in, wouldn't you? Five or six years old, a little blonde angel, you'd have given me your bread and honey and your Marmite soldiers and a big slice of cherry cake.'

Then, unable to keep up the self-mocking pretence another minute, he reached for a log, using it to stir the fire into life before tossing it into the heart of the flames, giving himself a moment or two to recover. He added a second log, then, his smile firmly in place, he risked another glance.

'You'd have defied your father, even when he threatened to chase me off with his shotgun.'

Charmed by this imagined image of a family gathered around the fire at teatime, he'd meant only to tease, but in an instant her smile faded to a look of such sadness that if he'd had a heart to break it would have shattered at her feet.

'You'd have been quite safe from my father, Tom. He was never at home on Sunday afternoon. It was always tea for two.'

Beneath her calm delivery he sensed pain and, remembering how swiftly she'd cut her father out of his role at her wedding this morning, a world of betrayal. A little girl should be able to count on her father. Look up to him. That she hadn't, she didn't, could only mean one thing.

'He was having an affair?'

'My mother must have known, realised the truth very soon after the big society wedding, but she protected me. Protected him.' She looked away, into the depths of the fire. 'She loved him, you see.'

It took him a minute, but he got there. 'Your father was gay?'

'Still is,' she said. 'A fact that I only learned when his own father died, at which point he stopped pretending to be the perfect husband and father and went with his lover to live on one of the

Greek islands, despite the fact that my mother had just been diagnosed with breast cancer. He didn't care what anyone else thought. It was only his father whose feelings he cared about.'

'If she loved him, Sylvie, I'm sure your mother was glad that he was finally able to be himself.'

'She said that, but she needed him. It was cruel to leave her.'

'Are you sure it wasn't actually a relief for her too? When you're sick you need all your energy just to survive.'

She swallowed. Just shook her head.

'Do you ever see him?' he persisted. And when silence answered that question, 'Does he want to see you?'

She gave an awkward little shrug. 'He sends birthday and Christmas cards through the family solicitor. I return them unopened.'

'No…'

Touched on the raw, the word escaped him. She did that to him. Loosed emotions, stirred memories. Now she was looking at him, her beautiful forehead puckered in a tiny frown, waiting for him to continue, and he closed out the bleak memories—this was not about him.

'He doesn't know he's going to be a grandfather in a few months?' he asked. 'Are you waiting for him to read an announcement in *The Times?* To Sylvie Duchamp Smith…' he couldn't bring himself to say Hillyer '…a son.'

Or had he, too, read about it in *Celebrity?* He remembered the shock of it. The unexpected pain…

There had been a moment then, when the idea of coming home had seemed so utterly pointless that he couldn't move. An emptiness that he hadn't experienced since the day he'd realised that his mother was never coming back and he was completely alone…

'A daughter,' she said, laying a protective hand over the curve of her abdomen. 'The scan showed that it's a girl.'

'…a daughter,' he said softly.

A little girl who'd have blonde curls and blue eyes and a smile to break a father's heart.

'I wonder how he'll feel when he hears,' he said, but only because he wanted her to think about it.

He already knew.

Cut out, shut off from something he could never be a part of.

'You care?' she demanded, astonished. Looking at him as if she couldn't believe what she was hearing. 'You're actually concerned?'

'Yes, Sylvie, I'm concerned. He's your father. His heart will break.'

Under the flush of heat from the fire, she went white.

'How dare you?' she said, gathering herself, pushing herself out of the chair, swaying slightly.

'Sylvie, I'm sorry…' He scrambled to his feet, reaching out to steady her, aware that he'd strayed into a minefield but too late to do more than apologise. This was all strange to him. He'd wanted, just for a moment, to share her happy childhood memories, not drag up bad ones.

It had never occurred to him that she could have had anything but the perfect childhood.

'Sorry? Is that it?' she said, shaking him off. 'You've got some kind of nerve, Tom McFarlane.' And she was striding to the door while he was still trying to work out what he'd done that was so awful.

Abandoning him to his foolish fantasies of happy families.

'Sylvie, please…' He was at the door before she reached it, blocking her way.

She refused to look at him, to speak to him. Just waited for him to recall his manners and let her pass, but he couldn't do that. Not until he'd said the words that were sitting like a lump in his throat.

He'd already apologised for the helpless, angry insult that had spilled from his lips earlier that morning—rare enough—but now he found himself apologising again, even though he didn't know why. Would have said anything if only she'd look at him, talk to him, stay…

'I'm sorry. It's none of my business…'

She looked up at the ceiling, determinedly ignoring him, but her eyes were suspiciously bright and he wanted to take her, sweep her into his arms, hold her, reassure her. Protect her from making what seemed to him to be the biggest mistake of her life.

Marrying Jeremy Hillyer *had* to be a mistake. He'd let her down once and he'd do it again.

She didn't have to marry him just because she was having his baby.

Or was that it?

Was she so desperate to give her baby something that she felt she'd been denied? If so, she was wrong. Her father may not have been the ideal 'daddy'; her childhood may not have been quite the picture book perfect life that he'd imagined. To go with this picture book house. But she did have a father and he knew exactly how the man must feel every time one of his letters or cards came back marked 'Return to Sender'.

'You lost your mother, Sylvie. You can't bring her back, but you still have a father. Don't let anger and pride keep you from him.'

'Don't!' She turned on him, eyes blazing, and he took a step back in the face of an anger so palpable that it felt like a punch on the jaw.

For a moment he thought she was going to say more, but she just shook her head and he said, 'What?'

'Just don't!' And now the tears were threatening to spill over, but even as he reached for her, determined to take her back to the fire where he could hold her so that she could cry, get it out of her system, she took a step back and said, 'Don't be such a damn hypocrite.'

She didn't wait for a response, but wrenched open the door and was gone from him, running up the stairs, leaving him to try and work out what he'd said that had made her so angry.

Hypocrite? Where had that come from?

All he'd done was encourage her to get in touch with her father. The birth of a baby was a time for new beginnings, a good time to bury old quarrels. She might not want to hear that, but how did saying it make him a hypocrite?

He was halfway up the stairs, determined to demand an answer, before reality brought him crashing to a halt.

She might have responded to his kiss, be anything but immune to the hot wire that seemed to run between them, but she was still pregnant with Jeremy Hillyer's child.

Was still going to marry the boy next door.

Sylvie gained the sanctuary of her bedroom and leaned against the door, breathing heavily, tears stinging against lids blocking out the fast fading light.

How could a man with such fire in his eyes, whose simplest kiss could dissolve her bones and who, with a touch could sear her to the soul, be so *cold*?

How *dared* he disapprove of the way she'd shut her father out of her life when he was refusing to acknowledge his own child?

Not by one word, one gesture, had he indicated that he was in any way interested. She could live with that for herself, but what had an innocent, unborn child done to merit such treatment?

She'd accepted, completely and sincerely, that the decision to have his baby had been entirely hers. She could have taken the morning-after pill. Had a termination. She had not consulted him but had taken the responsibility on herself and because of that she'd given him the chance to walk away. Forget it had ever happened.

No blame, no foul.

It was only now, confronted with the reality of what that really meant, did she fully understand how much she'd hoped for a different outcome.

She'd hoped, believed, that by removing everything from the equation but the fact that he was about to become a father, he'd be able to love his little girl as an unexpected gift.

How dumb could she be? At least if she'd sent in the lawyers, gone after him for maintenance, he'd have been forced to confront reality, would have become engaged with his daughter if only on a financial level. He'd demand contact fast enough then.

The billionaire entrepreneur who'd checked every item on the account would want value for money.

'Damn him,' she said, angrily swiping away the dampness that clung to her lashes with the heels of her hands. Then laid them gently over her baby and whispered, 'I'm so sorry, sweetheart. I messed up. Got it wrong.'

A bit of a family failing, that. But her mother hadn't fallen apart when life had dealt her a tricky hand. She'd handled it all with dignity, courage, humour.

Her marriage. Cancer. Even the loss of everything she'd held dear.

All that and with love and understanding too. Always with love. Especially for the unhappy man she'd fallen in love with and married. A man who'd loved his own father so much he'd lived a lie rather than 'come out' and bring the old reactionary's world crashing down. Who had loved her too.

How could Tom McFarlane be so right about that and so wrong about everything else?

'What'll I do, Mum?' she whispered. 'What would you do?'

* * *

Work had always been the answer. Fingers might get burned when a deal went wrong, but the heart remained unscathed, so Tom did what he always did when nothing else made sense. He returned to the library; not to the warmth of the fire but to the huge antique desk and the package of documents and personal stuff that had piled up while he'd been away and which Pam had couriered back from the office so that he could catch up with ongoing projects and set to work.

She'd even included the 'Coming Next Month' page from the latest edition of *Celebrity,* where a photograph of Longbourne Court promoted the 'world's favourite wedding planner's personal fantasy wedding' from The Pink Ribbon Club's Wedding Fayre.

He bit down hard, pushed it away so hard that it slid on to the floor along with a load of other stuff. He left it, intent on tossing away out of date invitations, letters from organisations asking him to speak, donate, join their boards. Clearing out the debris so that he could get back to what he knew. Making money.

That had been the centre of his world, the driving force that had kept him going for as long as he could remember.

But for what? What was the point of it all?

Losing patience, he dumped the lot in the bin. Anything to do with business would have been dealt with by his PA. Anything else and they'd no doubt write again.

He scooped up everything that had fallen on the floor and pitched that in too. About to crush the sheet from *Celebrity,* however, something stopped him.

Sylvie didn't dare linger too long in the bath in case she went to sleep. Having given herself no longer than it took for the lavender oil to do its soothing job, she climbed out, applied oil to her stomach and thighs to help stave off the dreaded stretch marks, then, wearing nothing but a towelling robe, she opened the bathroom door.

Tom McFarlane was propped up on one side of her bed.

All the warm, soothing effects of the lavender dissipated in an instant.

'Don't tell me,' she said icily. 'The Duchamp ghosts are after your blood.'

'Not that I've noticed,' he said. Then, 'I did knock.'

'And when did I say "come in"?' she demanded. 'I could have been naked!'

'In an English country house in April? How likely is that?'

'What do you want, Tom?'

'Nothing. I've had an idea.' And he patted the bed beside him, encouraging her to join him.

'And it couldn't keep until morning?' she protested, but sat on the edge of the bed. 'What kind of idea?'

'For your wedding.' He held up a page from *Celebrity* and she leaned forward to take a closer look.

'It's Longbourne Court. So?'

'Turn it over.'

She scanned the page. Could see nothing. 'Do you mean this advertisement for the Steam Museum in Lower Longbourne?' she said, easing her back. Wishing he'd get to the point so that she could lie down. 'It's just across the park. Big local attraction. So what?'

'Why don't you make yourself comfortable while you think about it?' he said, piling up her pillows and, when she hesitated, 'It's just like a sofa, only longer,' he said, clearly reading her mind.

She wasn't sure she'd feel safe on a sofa with him but it was clear he wasn't saying another word until she was sitting comfortably so she tugged the robe around her and sat back, primly, against the pillows.

'Okay,' she said. 'The Steam Museum. At Hillyer House.

Jeremy's grandfather was mad about steam engines and gathered them up as they went out of use. He worked on them himself, restoring them, had open days so that the public could enjoy them. I loved the carousels—'

'They're not carousels, they're gallopers,' Tom said. 'They're called carousels on the Continent.' He made a circling motion with his hand. 'And they go round the other way.'

'Do they? Why?'

'It's to do with the fact that we drive on the left.' She stared at him. 'Honestly!'

'Don't tell me, you worked in a fairground.'

'I worked in a fairground,' he said.

'I told you not to tell me that…' she said, then looked hurriedly away. That was one of those silly things her father used to say to make her laugh.

'Okay, *gallopers,* rides, swings. It's set up just like a real old-fashioned steam fair…' She clapped her hands to her mouth. Then grinned. 'Ohmigod. Wedding Fayre… Steam fair…'

Sylvie laughed as the sheer brilliance of the idea hit her. 'It's the perfect theme, Tom,' she said as the ideas flooded in. 'You're a genius!'

'I know, but hadn't you better clear it with Jeremy first?'

'Jeremy? No. There's no need for that…' Steam engines had been the old Earl's pet obsession; Jeremy had never been interested—much too slow for him and it was run by a Trust these days. 'It even fits in with the idea of promoting local businesses.'

'Well, that's all right, then,' he said.

She glanced at him. 'What?'

He shook his head. 'Nothing. As you say, it all fits beautifully.'

'They've got everything. Test your strength. Bowl for the pig—just pottery ones, but they're lovely. And made locally too. There are even hay-cart rides to take visitors around the place.'

'I guess the big question is—does it beat the elephant?'

'Too right!' She drew up her legs, wrapping her arms around them. 'The photographer could use one of those things where you stick your head through the hole—'

'A bride and groom one.'

'—for all the guests to have their photographs taken.'

She couldn't stop grinning. 'We'll decorate the marquee with ribbons and coloured lights instead of flowers. And set up sideshow stalls for the food.' She looked at him. 'Bangers and mash?'

He grinned back. 'Fish and chips. Hot dogs.'

'Candyfloss! And little individual cakes.' She'd intended to go for something incredibly tasteful, but nothing about this fantasy was going to be tasteful. It was going to be fun. With a capital F. 'I'll talk to the confectioner first thing. I want each one decorated with a fairground motif.'

Tom watched as, swept up in the sheer fun of it, she clapped her hands over her mouth like a child wanting to hold it in, savour every minute of it.

'You like it?' he asked.

'Like it!' She turned and, anger forgotten, she flung her arms around him, hugging him in her excitement. 'You're brilliant. I don't suppose you're looking for a job?' Then, before he could answer, 'Sorry, sorry… Genius billionaire. Why would you want to work for me? Damn, I wish it wasn't all such a rush.'

'Is it even possible in the time?'

'Oh, yes.'

He must have looked doubtful because she said, 'Piece of cake. Honestly.'

Of course it was. The Steam Museum had been created by Lord Hillyer. All she had to do was ask and it would be hers for the day.

'Now I know what I want it'll all just fall into place, although I could have done with Josie to sort out the marquee. That's going to be the biggest job.'

'If it helps, you've got me.'

They were on her bed and she had her arms around him and he was telling her what was in his heart, but only he knew that. Only he would ever know that she'd got him—totally, completely, in ways that had nothing to do with sex but everything to do with a word that he didn't even begin to understand, but knew with every fibre of his being that this was it. The real deal.

Giving without hope of ever receiving back.

Sylvie's mother would have understood. Would know how he was feeling.

Sylvie… Sylvie was nearly there. Maybe his true gift to her would be to help her make that final leap…

'You'd be willing to help?' she asked, leaning back, a tiny frown puckering her brow.

He shrugged, pulled a face. 'You said it. The sooner you're done, the sooner you're out of here.'

'That's it?' She drew back as if his answer shocked her. As if she'd expected something more.

But that was it.

More was beyond him.

'I want my house back and, to get it, I'm prepared to put all my resources at your disposal,' he said with all the carelessness he could muster.

Maybe just one thing more…

'There's just one condition.' Then, as the colour flooded into her cheeks, he said, 'No!'

Yes…

'No,' he repeated. 'All I want from you is that you write to your father.'

'No…' The word came out as a whisper.

'Yes! Ask him to share the day with you. Let him into your little girl's life.'

'Why?' she demanded. 'Why do you care about him?'

More and more and more…

'Because… Because I know what it's like to have letters returned unopened. Because one day when I was four years old people came and took my mother away. I hung on to her and that was the only time I saw her cry. As she pulled away, leaving me to the waiting social workers. "I'll be all right," she said. "I have to go. These people will look after you until I come home…"'

Then, helplessly, 'You said you'd have my story.'

'Where was your father, Tom?'

'Dead. She'd killed him. A battered woman who'd finally struck back, using the first thing that came to hand. A kitchen knife.' Then, more urgently, because this was what he had to do to make sure she understood, 'They took her away, put me in care. I didn't understand. I wrote to her, begging her to come and get me. Week after week. And week after week the letters just came back…'

She said nothing, just held him, as if she could make it all better. And maybe she had. Her need had dragged the story out of him. Had made him say the words. Had made him see that it wasn't his fault that his mother had died too.

'I'm sure she thought it was for the best that I forgot her, moved on, found a new family.'

'But you didn't.'

'She was my mother, Sylvie. She might not have been the greatest mother in the world, but she was the only one I ever wanted.'

Sylvie thought her heart might break at the thought of a little boy writing his desperate letters, having them returned unopened. Understood his empathy for her own father.

'What happened to her, Tom?'

'She never stood trial. By the time her case eventually came up she was beyond the law, in some dark place in her mind. She should have been in hospital, not prison. Maybe there she'd have got help instead of taking her own life.'

She reached out a hand to him. Almost, but not quite, touched his cheek. Then said, 'Are you sure you haven't been visiting with the Duchamp ghosts?'

He'd had no way of knowing how she'd react to the fact that he was the son of a wife-batterer, a husband-killer. A suggestion that he'd been communing with her ancestors hadn't even made the list and, at something of a loss, he said, 'Why would you think that?'

'Because I asked my mother what she'd do. I already knew the answer. Have always known it. Maybe she thought it was time to get someone else on my case…'

And finally her fingers came into contact with his cheek, as if by touching him she was reaching through him to her mother. And, just as they had on the evening when the connection between them had become physical, silent tears were pouring down her cheeks, but this time there was no one to interrupt them and she didn't push him away, but let him draw her close, hold her while he said, over and over, 'Don't cry, Sylvie,' even as his own tears soaked into her hair. 'Please don't cry.'

And eventually, when she quieted, drew back, it was she who wiped his cheeks with her fingers.

Comforted him.

'It'll be all right,' she said, holding his face between her hands. Kissing his cheek. 'I promise you, it'll be all right.'

'You'll write to him? Now?'

'It won't wait until morning?'

'What would your mother say?'

She sniffed and, laughing, swung herself from the bed to grab a tissue. 'Okay, okay, I'll do it.' Then, 'I'll have to fetch my bag; I left it downstairs.'

She crossed to the door, then, halfway through it, she paused and looked back. 'Tom?'

He waited.

'Don't make the same mistake your mother did.' She was cradling the life growing within her in a protective gesture. It was the most powerful instinct on earth. The drive of the mother to protect her young. His mother had done that. Had protected him from his father. Had protected him from herself…

'You're more than your genes,' she said when he didn't respond. 'You've forged your own character. It's strong and true and, I promise you, you're the kind of father any little girl would want.'

There was an urgency in her voice. A touch of desperation. As if she knew that her own baby wouldn't be that lucky…

He couldn't help her. If it had been in his power he would have stopped the world and spun it back to give them both a second chance to get things right. But he couldn't help either of them.

CHAPTER TEN

SYLVIE finally began to understand what was driving Tom's inability to make an emotional commitment. How hard it must be for him to trust not just himself, but anyone.

To understand his anger, his pain at Candy's desertion. He might not have loved her, but she'd still underscored all that early imprinting. That early lesson that no one was to be relied on…

And yet he'd trusted her enough, cared enough to stop her from hurting someone who she knew, deep down, loved her. That was a huge step forward.

She'd done her best to reassure him that he was not his father, or his mother. If she'd hoped that he'd instantly come over all paternal, well, that was unrealistic. He'd had a lifetime to live with the horrors of his early life, for the certainty that he did not want children to become ingrained into his psyche. He couldn't be expected to switch all that off in a moment.

But the longest journey started with a single step. Tonight they'd made that together.

Tom was using his cellphone when she returned to the bedroom, talking to someone about making the sideshow booths. He lifted a hand in acknowledgement and carried on, while she opened her bag, took out the small folder of notepaper she kept in there and settled at the small escritoire to write her letter. The second most difficult in her life.

It was a deliberate ploy. She wanted him to see her pen gliding across the same heavy cream paper on which she'd written to him. She uncapped her pen and smoothed a hand over her hair, lingering at the damp patch where his tears had soaked in.

And then, pushing all that from her mind, she began.

'That didn't take long,' Tom said, watching as she carefully folded the sheet into four and tucked it into an envelope. Addressed it.

'No. Sometimes things you think are impossible are nowhere near as difficult as you imagine,' she said and looked up as he joined her. 'I just invited Dad and his partner to join the festivities on Sunday. It was as simple as that.'

'Will it get there in time?'

'I'll take it to the post office first thing in the morning and send it express.'

'You'll have enough to do,' he said, holding out his hand for it. 'Leave it to me.'

'Thank you,' she said and placed the envelope in his hands. Would he remember the feel of it? How he'd felt when he'd opened it?

'I've organised a carpenter to build the stalls for the marquee,' he said. 'They'll be here first thing.'

'Fast work.' She glanced at her watch. It was barely nine. Still early enough to call some of those people who'd assured her that she could call any time, ask anything.

'What about the Steam Museum? I imagine you'll want to sort that out personally?'

'The sooner the better. I'll make that call first.'

As she picked up her cellphone Tom headed for the door. 'I'll leave you to it, then. You can leave this with me.'

He didn't wait for her to reply but, lifting the letter to indicate what he was referring to, he left her alone.

It was somewhat abrupt but it had been an emotion-charged evening. Maybe he just needed some air.

And she let it go, calling Laura, who knew everyone, and handing her the job of securing the Steam Museum for the photo shoot.

It didn't open until two on Sunday so they had plenty of time. The church was booked for early afternoon. They could finish off in the marquee in the early evening.

Tom closed the door to Sylvie's bedroom, leaned back against it for a moment while he caught his breath. While she called Jeremy to enthuse him with her excitement. Got him to call the trustees and ask them for the loan of some of his grandfather's toys for their big day.

He looked down at the letter he was holding. At least he'd managed to save one man from heartache.

His own would have to wait. He'd made her a promise and he'd keep it. But he'd leave as soon as he was sure everything was just as she wanted it. He didn't intend to be an onlooker when Jeremy Hillyer arrived to claim his bride.

'It's beautiful, Geena.'

The dress, a simple A-line shift in rich cream silk, had been appliquéd to the knees in swirling blocks of lavender, purple and green. And, instead of a veil, she'd created a stunningly beautiful loose thigh-length jacket on which the appliqué was repeated around the edge and on wide fold-back cuffs. Embroidery trailed over the silk and tiny beads caught the light as she moved—beads that matched the small Russian-style tiara Geena had commissioned to go with the gown.

'I just wish it was for real. I really hoped you were going to bring Mr Hot-and-Sexy along to try on the matching waistcoat,' she said.

'Me too,' Sylvie replied, for once letting her mask slip, her feelings show. Then, 'I meant, I wish it was for real.'

'I know what you meant, Sylvie. It was written all over your face. He is your baby's father, isn't he?'

Sylvie tried to deny it. Couldn't. Lifted her hands in a helpless gesture that said it all.

'I thought so. Men are such fools.'

'We're all fools,' she said, shrugging off the beautiful jacket.

The week had been such a roller coaster of emotions that she was almost reeling from it. Or maybe she was just exhausted.

Tom had been such a tower of strength. Organising carpenters to make the food stalls. Rounding up every set of coloured lights in the county and making sure they were fixed for maximum impact so that inside the marquee was like being inside a funfair. Finding old fairground ride cars and adapting them for seating.

And, in the evenings, he was always there, ready to talk through any problems she'd encountered and offer suggestions.

He had such a clear vision, a way of seeing to the core of things.

He only had one blind spot. There was only one subject he never mentioned. It was almost as if he was so locked into his past, his determination never to be a father, that he'd blanked it out.

It couldn't go on.

She wouldn't allow it to go on.

'Is that the dress?'

Tom was working at the kitchen table as she walked in carrying the box containing the tissue-wrapped dress and he pushed back the chair, standing up to take it from her.

'Yes. I insisted on bringing it with me, just in case.'

'In case of what?'

'In case she has a flat tyre. Or her workroom burns to the ground.' The principle that whatever can go wrong, will go wrong. 'Believe me, when you've been in this business for as long as I have—'

'Actually, Sylvie, I'm a bit concerned about the traction engines. I know you said Laura had it all in hand, but shouldn't they—'

'You don't have to worry about them. We've got all morning,' she said. 'Plenty of time.' Then, 'I'll just take this upstairs, then I want to talk to you, Tom.'

'Can you leave it for a moment?' he asked, taking the box from her, putting it on the table. 'I want you to come and see the marquee.'

'I thought it was finished.'

'It is now,' he said with the kind of smile that had become such a familiar sight over the last few days as they'd worked together. And he held out his hand. 'I've got a surprise for you.'

She laid her hand over his and he wrapped his fingers over hers. For a moment neither of them moved, then, as if jerking himself back from a dream, he headed for the door. Once they were outside, he paused for her to fall in beside him and they walked together, hand in hand, through the dusk to where the huge marquee had been erected by the hire company to display their wares, decorated at *Celebrity*'s expense for her fantasy wedding.

'Wait,' he said as they approached the entrance. 'I want you to get the full effect.' He kept tight hold of her hand as he switched on the generator. The outside was lit up with white lights along every edge—along the roof ridge, cascading from the finials, circling above the drop cloths.

Inside, the lights—smaller, more decorative, a mirror image of those on the outside—were reflecting on the polished floor. The supports were topped with huge knots of brightly coloured ribbons, the same ribbons that were plaited around them to the floor. In the corners were brightly painted stalls, offering a choice of foods. The fairground seating.

Small finishing touches had been added during the afternoon. The candyfloss machine had arrived. Bunches of balloons were straining against their strings.

And then, as she looked around, she saw it.

A fairground organ. The kind that played from printed sheets. He crossed to it, threw a switch and, as if by magic, it began to play, music filling the huge space.

'Tom! It's wonderful! The perfect finishing touch.'

Even as Sylvie said the words, she felt her skin rise in goose-bumps. Nothing was ever perfect…

But then Tom said, 'Would you care to dance, Miss Smith?' And, before she could protest, he was waltzing her across the floor. And it was. Magic.

About as perfect as it was possible for something to be.

And much too brief. The music stopped. Tom held her for just a moment longer. Then he stepped away.

'Enough.'

The word had a finality about it but, before she could say anything, he turned away. 'Go in, Sylvie. It'll take me a while to shut everything down. Make sure it's all safe. I'll leave the lights until last so that you can see your way.' Then, 'Take care.'

'Yes, I will.'

For a moment neither of them moved and then, because the longer she hesitated, the longer it would be before he could join her and she could talk to him about the future, she turned and walked back to the house.

Inside, the hall was now festooned with pink ribbons in prep-aration for tomorrow's Fayre. The door to the ballroom stood wide open to reveal the catwalk, the tables with gilt chairs laid out in preparation for the fashion show. Mother of the bride outfits, going-away outfits, honeymoon clothes. Formal hire wear for men, including kilts. Bridesmaids and page-boy outfits. And, finally, Geena's bridal wear.

The florist had been busy all day putting the finishing touches to her arrangements. Pew-end nosegays that had been hung all along the edge of the catwalk. Table flowers.

In the drawing room all the stalls were laid out like an Aladdin's cave. Everything sparkling, fresh, lovely.

Laura was right. This was worth it, she thought. Even the weather forecast was good. It was going to be warm and sunny as it had been all week.

So why was she so cold?

She pushed open the library door, eager to get to the fire she knew would be banked up behind the guard.

But the guard was down. The room was not empty. There was someone sitting in Tom's chair. A man, who stood up as she came to an abrupt halt.

Her father.

Older, with a little less hair, a little thicker around the waist-line. Deeply tanned. Still unbelievably good-looking.

Waiting. Uncertain.

She took a step towards him. He took one towards her and then she reached out, took his hand and carried it to her waist. 'You're going to be a grandfather,' she said.

'I read about it in *Celebrity*. When I saw the photograph I thought for one awful moment you were back with that piece of…' he stopped '…Jeremy Hillyer. I thought you were back with him.'

'It's not Jeremy's baby.' She covered his hand with her own. 'It's Tom's baby.' Then, 'He knew you were here, didn't he? That's why he sent me on ahead of him.'

'He said he thought we might need some time on our own.'

Then, 'I'd given up hope. When I read about the baby and you still didn't get in touch, I knew it would never happen.'

'I'm sorry. So sorry…'

'Hush. You're my little girl, Sylvie. You don't ever have to say you're sorry.' And he put out his arms and gathered her in.

Later—after they'd both cried as they'd talked about her mother, as they'd discovered they could laugh too—she said, 'Did you bring Michael with you?'

'We're staying in Melchester. He'll come tomorrow. Thank you for asking him.'

'You love him. He's part of our lives.'

'And Tom? Is he going to be part of yours?'

'I…I don't know. Just when I think that maybe it's going to be all right, I realise it isn't.' And she shivered again.

'Maybe you should go and find him, Sylvie. We can talk some more tomorrow.'

'Tom?'

She'd watched her father's tail-lights disappear over the brow of the hill and then walked through the house looking for Tom. Not just to thank him, but determined now, as never before, to make him see reason about the baby.

Mrs Kennedy was in the kitchen making a sandwich. 'Tom asked me to make sure you had something to eat.'

'I had some soup.'

'Hours ago. Did you have a visitor?'

'My father. He's coming for the Fayre tomorrow. He hopes to see you.'

'I should think so.' And she smiled. 'I'm glad you've made up.'

'Yes. Me too.' Then, 'Where is Tom?'

'As to that, I couldn't say,' she said, wiping her hands and reaching up behind a plate on the dresser to take down an envelope. 'But he called in to the cottage on his way out and asked me to come over in an hour or two and make sure you had something to eat. He said to tell you he left something upstairs for you. In your room.'

'On his way out? When?'

'A while back. Just after he turned out the lights in the marquee.'

She checked her watch. Nearer two hours. She'd thought Tom was just staying out of the way, giving them time to talk.

But she remembered the way she'd shivered. The finality in the way he'd said, 'Enough'. That he'd left something upstairs for her. Something he hadn't wanted her to find before he'd left...

She bolted up the stairs, flung open her bedroom door and saw the clown teddy propped up on her bed, just where Tom had been lying a few days ago. Looking for all the world as if he belonged there.

Because he had.

She picked up the bear, knowing that Tom had taken it from the trunk, carried it down to her room, placed it there. She buried her face in it, hoping to catch something of his scent. Trying to feel him, understand what had been going through his mind as he'd been putting things right for her. For her family.

Just as, all week, he'd been making things work for her fantasy wedding. Coming up with neat little ideas to part the visitors to the Wedding Fayre from their money. All little extras for the Pink Ribbon Club.

Then, as she looked up, she saw the letter that had been lying beneath the bear and she ripped open the flap, took out the single folded sheet of paper, then sat down before she opened it, knowing it wouldn't be good.

My dearest Sylvie

*Tomorrow will be your very special day and, now you have
your father to support you, I know I can leave you in his
safe hands.*

*I'm going away for a while—but not running this time.
I need to find something new to do with my life. Something
bigger. Something real. My first decision is not to convert
the house into a conference centre. It's a real home and I
hope it will remain as such. Whatever happens, you needn't
worry about Mr and Mrs Kennedy. I've made arrangements to ensure they'll never have to leave their home.*

*I've also asked Mrs Kennedy to see that all the clothes
in the attic are donated to Melchester Museum. Everything
else of value in the trunks is to be given to the Pink Ribbon
Club for fund-raising purposes. The bear, however, is
yours. Something belonging to your family that you can
pass on to your own baby.*

*Finally, I want to reassure you that you can rely on my
discretion. What happened between us will always remain
a very special, a very private memory.*

*I hope the sun shines for you tomorrow and wish you
and Jeremy a long and happy life together.*

Yours

Tom

Sylvie read the note. Maybe she was tired; she was certainly
emotionally drained, but none of it made sense.

She'd seen him just a couple of hours ago. And what the heck
did he mean about her having a long and happy life with Jeremy?

She read the letter again, then went back down to the kitchen.

'What does Tom mean about you never having to leave your
home, Mrs Kennedy?'

She smiled. 'Bless the man, he gave it to us. Said that's what Lady Annika would have done if she'd been able to and anyway it wouldn't be missed from the estate when it was sold.'

Sylvie sat down.

He'd given it to them. Just because she'd said… 'And the clothes? You're to send them to the Museum?'

'I believe he spoke to someone there just yesterday. He said to tell you that if there's anything you want, you should take it.'

She shook her head. 'No…'

He'd been planning this? Why hadn't he said anything?

She re-read the last paragraph again:

"…I hope the sun shines for you tomorrow, and wish you and Jeremy a long and happy life together."

Jeremy?

He was always bringing up Jeremy. Had even mentioned seeing them in *Celebrity* together. Had the entire world seen that? Even her father had said…

Oh, good grief. No. He couldn't possibly think that all this wedding stuff was real. Could he?

Did he really believe that she was marrying Jeremy while she was carrying his baby? While she had been practically swooning in his arms in the attics? Was that why he'd pulled back from that kiss over the kitchen table?

"…you can rely on my discretion…"

Was that what he thought she'd wanted to talk to him about? To plead for his discretion?

'Oh, no, Tom McFarlane, you don't…'

She had his cellphone number programmed into her phone and she hit fast dial but his phone was turned off and all she got was some anonymous voice inviting her to leave a message.

'Tom? Don't you dare do another disappearing act on me—not until you've spoken to me! Ring me, do you hear? Ring me now!'

But what if he didn't?

What if he decided to head straight for the airport, put as much distance between them as possible? It was what he'd done when Candy had let him down.

She froze. Was it possible that he'd only just come back? That he'd never received her letter?

No. That wasn't possible. Despite her promise to him—to herself—she'd cracked, had asked him if he'd got it. She'd never forget his dismissive nod. And a long time later, "I'm sorry…"

None of this made sense. She had to talk to him. She dialled Enquiries for the number of his London apartment, but inevitably, it was unlisted. And there was no point in calling his office on a Saturday night. But she did that too. If he was there he didn't pick up.

There was nothing for it but to drive to London and confront him, face to face. Scooping up one of the sandwiches Mrs Kennedy had made and grabbing up her keys from the kitchen table, she ran for her car.

Tom let himself into his apartment. It was immaculate. Everything was pristine. Characterless. Empty.

As different from Longbourne Court as it was possible for it to be. In a week that rambling house had become his home. A place where he felt totally at ease.

But it would be forever linked to Sylvie. Everything he touched, every room, would bring back some memory of a smile, a gesture.

He'd never be able to walk into the morning room without remembering what he'd said to her.

Would never see violets blooming in the wood without the scent bringing back that moment when he'd come so close to reaching out to her. Betraying himself.

He tossed the keys on the table. Rubbed his hands over his face in an attempt to bring some life, some warmth back to his skin.

Picked up one of the piles of mail that his cleaner had put to one side. She'd clearly tossed everything that was obviously junk mail and had sorted the rest into two piles. The stuff she knew was important she'd put in one, anything she was doubtful about in the other.

There wasn't that much, considering how long it was since he'd been home, but all his business and financial stuff went to the office and most of his personal stuff too.

He began to shuffle through the envelopes, lost interest and tossed them back on the table, where they slithered on the polished surface and fell on the floor.

About to walk past, leave them, he saw a familiar square cream envelope, took a step back and then bent to pick it up.

It might have been coincidence that it was exactly the same as the envelope that he'd taken to the post office for Sylvie. It might have been if the handwriting hadn't been the same.

When had she written to him?

There was no stamp. No postmark. No way of knowing how long it had lain here waiting for him to return. She must have delivered it by hand. She must have come here, pushed it through his letter box, waited for an answer that had never come.

She'd asked him if he'd got her letter and he'd thought she'd meant the one returning the money but he knew that it was this letter she'd been talking about and, with a sudden sense of dread, he pushed his thumb beneath the flap and, hand trembling, took out the single sheet of paper and opened it.

Dear Mr McFarlane
I'm writing to let you know that as a result of our recent
encounter, I'm expecting a baby in July…

'No!'

The word was a roar. A bellow of pain.

He didn't wait to read the rest but grabbed the phone, put a call through to the house. It rang and rang and then the answering machine picked up. 'There's to be no damn wedding tomorrow,' he said. 'Do you hear me, Sylvie? No wedding!'

Then he tried her cellphone, but only got a voicemail prompt. He repeated his message, then added, 'I'm coming right back…'

Then, in desperation, he called the Kennedys' cottage.

Her car refused to start. Her beloved, precious little car that had never once let her down, chose this moment to play dead. The lights. She'd driven through a patch of mist and had turned the lights on. And had forgotten to turn them off.

It took her ten minutes at a trot to reach the Kennedys' cottage.

'Don't you fret, Sylvie,' Mrs Kennedy said. 'You just sit down and I'll make you a cup of tea. Mr Kennedy's at a darts match, but the minute he comes home he'll get his jump-leads and fix your car for you.'

'I can't wait. I'll have to call a taxi.'

'I'll do that while you get your breath back.'

There was a half an hour wait and, while Mrs Kennedy went off to make 'a nice cup of tea', she decided to try and call Tom again, but her phone, which had been working overtime all day, chose that moment to join her car and give up the ghost.

'Stupid, useless thing,' she said, flinging it back into her bag, too angry to cry.

It was nearer an hour before she heard the taxi finally draw up outside the cottage and she didn't wait for the driver to knock but just grabbed her bag, kissed Mrs Kennedy and ran down the path to the gate.

And came to a full stop.

Leaning against the fearsome Aston, arms folded, was Tom McFarlane. And he didn't look happy.

She opened her mouth. Saw what he was holding and closed it again.

Apparently satisfied, he straightened, opened the car door and said, 'Get in.'

He didn't sound happy either and while, as recently as sixty seconds ago, she'd been fuming with impatience to see him, talk to him, that suddenly felt like the most dangerous idea in the entire world.

'You've got everything wrong, Tom,' she said, her feet apparently glued to the path.

'Nowhere near as wrong as you, Sylvie.'

'I don't actually think that's possible,' she said, finally snapping.

He was angry? Well, she wasn't exactly dancing with delight either and, freed by righteous indignation, she swept down the path and, ignoring the open car door, she walked away from him and his car. She'd rather walk…

'Sylvie!' It was a demand rather than a plea. Then, with a sudden catch in his throat, 'Sylvie, don't do it…' She faltered. 'I'm begging you. Please…'

She stopped and, when he spoke again, he was right behind her.

'Please don't marry Jeremy Hillyer.'

It was true, then. He'd really thought she was going to marry Jeremy.

'But you've been helping me all week,' she said. 'Coming up with great ideas for the wedding. This afternoon you wrote me a note wishing us all the best. What's different now?'

'Everything. I thought the baby was his. I was coming home two months ago. Coming to see you. I didn't know if you'd even talk to me but I had to try. I was in the airport, the boarding card in my pocket when I saw you smiling out of the cover of *Celebrity*. Read about your "happy event", that you were back with your childhood sweetheart.'

'But I wrote to you, Tom. I told you about the baby. I asked you if you'd got it.'

'I thought you meant the one about the money. My secretary emailed me to tell me that you'd returned it, asking me what to do with it, and I realised what you must have thought. It wasn't like that, Sylvie. I'd always intended to pay you in full. The cheque I wrote, put in my pocket, was for your whole fee.'

'Oh.'

'I told her to give it to charity, if that's any consolation.' Then, 'I didn't get this letter until this evening, Sylvie. I didn't know about our little girl…'

She blinked. 'That's impossible. I put it through your door myself. Two weeks after…' She gestured helplessly at the gentle swell of her belly.

'Which would have been perfect if I'd been there. I've been out of the country for six months, Sylvie. I only stopped to pick up my passport and then I caught the first plane with a free seat, just to put some space between us.'

'Um…I thought you were going to Mustique…'

'How could I go there after you and I…?' And he was the one lost for words. 'I hurt you, Sylvie. Made you cry. I've only made two women cry in my entire life.'

'Your mother…'

"I'll be all right. I have to go…"

His mother had said that. And so had she…

'I was crying because you'd given me something so unbeliev-able, Tom. I'd been frozen, held in an emotional Ice Age. Too much had happened at once. I'd lost everything and then been betrayed…' She looked up at him, wanting him to know that this was the truth. 'I spent my life making perfect weddings for other people when I was unable to even share a kiss…'

'Sylvie…'

'I came straight back, as soon as I could, but you'd gone.'

'I was in bits. I thought you couldn't wait to leave… Never wanted to set eyes on me again and who could blame you?'

She reached up, placed her fingers over his lips. 'You are my sun, Tom. You looked at me and it was instant meltdown. You held me and your heat warmed me.'

'But…'

'The tears were pure joy, Tom. And the baby…' She took his hand and placed it over the baby growing beneath her heart. '*Our* baby is pure joy too.'

'She's mine…' His face, pale in the rising moon, glowed with something like reverence. 'My little girl.'

She'd cried then and she was crying now. Silent tears that were falling down her cheeks as she said, 'You have a family, Tom.'

For a moment they just stood there and then he said, 'It's not enough. I want you, Sylvie. I tried to get you out of my mind, tried to forget you, but it was no good. I…' He stopped.

'You what, Tom?' She reached up, her palms on his cheeks, making him look at her when he would have turned away. 'Say the words.'

'I…I love you.' Then, 'I love you, but I've made a complete mess of it. It's too late…'

'Because of the wedding tomorrow? Is that the only thing standing between us?'

'Sylvie…' And this time her name was a tortured cry that rent her to the heart.

'It's a fantasy wedding, Tom. Not real. Just the "Sylvie Duchamp Smith" fantasy of what her wedding would be. If…when…she ever found a man she could spend the rest of her life with.'

She saw him wrestle with that.

'But Jeremy…'

'Is not that man. We met at a charity do. We were polite, we smiled at each other. *Celebrity* did the rest. I suspect they were hoping to provoke me into naming the real father of my child.'

'But you've been ordering cakes. Food. Flowers. You've got an updated version of the dress you were going to wear the first time…'

'The dress is nothing like the one that my great-grandma wore,' she assured him. 'I have an entirely different fantasy these days.' Then, 'I can't believe you'd think I'd sell my own wedding to the media.'

'I had the impression that you'd do anything for your mother's charity.'

'Some things are not for sale, Tom.'

Then, catching a flicker of light, the twitch of a curtain from the Kennedys' cottage, she said, 'They knew, didn't they? They knew you were coming back.'

'If you'd turned on your cellphone any time in the last two hours, so would you.'

'My battery is flat. What did you say?'

'"There will be no wedding…"'

'None?'

'Not tomorrow,' he said, reaching out and touching her cheek. 'But soon, I hope. Very soon. Because if you think you can have my baby without any expectation of commitment to her father, you've got another think coming.'

'Is that right?'

'And it's my fantasy too, remember? I want the whole works.'

'All of it?'

'All of it. Everything, everyone. Except *Celebrity*. They can have their fantasy tomorrow, but the reality will be for us alone. Not just for a day, but for always.' Then, as if realising that something was missing, he went down on one knee and, under a bright canopy of stars, he said, 'If I promise to wear a purple waistcoat to match your shoes, will you marry me, Sylvie Smith?'

Four weeks after the Pink Ribbon Club Wedding Fayre featuring Sylvie Duchamp Smith's fantasy wedding was a sell-out for *Celebrity*, Tom and Sylvie did it for real.

Sylvie arrived at the church on a traction engine that was all gleaming paintwork and brass. Geena had made her another dress—since, obviously, the groom had seen the first one. It wasn't quite the same since she never repeated her designer gowns, but it was close. And Sylvie wore the purple shoes.

Josie had added a dusting of green glitter to her purple hair and, having been bribed with an appliquéd dress with a tiny little matching jacket and a pair of pale green silk-embroidered shoes, had surrendered her boots.

The god-daughters were adorable in lavender and violet. The page scowled, but that was only to be expected. Even a five-year-old knew that purple velvet breeches were an outrage. And, as she walked up the aisle on the arm of her father, the sunlight caught the diamonds in the tiara Tom had commissioned from a local jeweller for his bride.

The fair was a riot, the food was pronounced perfect, the

children were sick on candyfloss—well, nothing was ever *quite* perfect—and Josie, now the partner in charge of weddings and parties, was overwhelmed with people demanding exactly the same for their own special day.

But, as Tom had told Sylvie, this was a one-off. For them alone.

nocturne™

THE FINAL INSTALLMENT OF
THE BLOODRUNNERS TRILOGY

Last Wolf Watching

Runner Brody Carter has found his match in
Michaela Doucet, a human with unusual psychic powers.
When Michaela's brother is threatened, Brody becomes
her protector, and suddenly not only has to protect her
from her enemies but also from himself....

LOOK FOR
LAST WOLF WATCHING
BY
RHYANNON
BYRD

Available May 2008 wherever you buy books.

Dramatic and Sensual Tales of Paranormal Romance

www.eHarlequin.com　　　　　SN61786

HARLEQUIN® *Romance*®

Western Weddings

Jason Welborn was convinced that his business partner's daughter, Jenny, had come to claim her share in the business. But Jenny seemed determined to win him over, and the more he tried to push her away, the more feisty Jenny's response. Slowly but surely she was starting to get under Jason's skin....

Look for

Coming Home to the Cattleman

by

JUDY CHRISTENBERRY

Available May wherever you buy books.

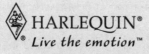

HARLEQUIN®

Live the emotion™

www.eHarlequin.com

HRI7511

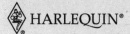

HARLEQUIN *Romance*

Coming Next Month

It's raining men this month at Harlequin Romance®, with a rancher, an Italian playboy, a sheikh boss, a Boston society heir, an entrepreneur to the rescue and a single dad to melt your heart!

#4021 COMING HOME TO THE CATTLEMAN Judy Christenberry
Western Weddings

What does home mean to you? For Jenny, it's a distant memory. But this time going home brings her into conflict with the aloof and brooding Jason, her dad's business partner, who has been less than welcoming....

#4022 THE ITALIAN PLAYBOY'S SECRET SON Rebecca Winters
Mediterranean Dads

In the second book of the spectacular duet, a terrifying crash has put race car driver Cesar Villon de Falcon in hospital, fighting for his life. Sarah has come to tell him a secret that will bring him back to life: he has a son!

#4023 THE HEIR'S CONVENIENT WIFE Myrna Mackenzie
The Wedding Planners

The series continues with more bridal fun! Photographer Regina realizes she hardly knows the man she conveniently wed. He may be strong, honorable and the heir to Boston's most distinguished business empire... but what about the man inside?

#4024 HER SHEIKH BOSS Carol Grace
Desert Brides

Duty is the most important thing in Sheikh Samir's life—an arranged marriage to a suitable woman was always his destiny. But then, on a business trip in the desert, Samir starts to see his sensible but spirited assistant Claudia in a whole new light....

#4025 WANTED: WHITE WEDDING Natasha Oakley

Do you dream of the perfect white wedding? Freya spent hours planning hers when she was young as a way to escape the troubles of home. Now she's made something of her life and all that's missing is someone to share it with—until she meets a gorgeous single dad....

#4026 HIS PREGNANT HOUSEKEEPER Caroline Anderson
Baby on Board

Wealthy architect Daniel can't turn his back on pregnant Iona, whom he finds penniless and alone in a building he is redeveloping. It's all her Cinderella fantasies come true when Daniel promises to take care of her. But can the fairy tale really last?

HRCNM0408